I0669866

BOOKED

For

CHRISTMAS

BOOKED

For

CHRISTMAS

LORE TOWNSEND

Booked for Christmas
Paperback Edition
Copyright © 2025 by Lore Townsend

Love N. Books Press
An Imprint of Wolfpack Publishing
1707 E. Diana Street
Tampa, FL 33610

www.lovenbookspress.com

All rights reserved. No part of this book may be reproduced in any form or by any electronic or mechanical means, including information storage and retrieval systems, without express written permission from the publisher, except for the use of brief quotations in reviews. Any use of this publication to train generative artificial intelligence (AI) technologies is expressly prohibited.

This book is a work of fiction. References to historical events, real people, or real places are used fictitiously. Any similarity to real persons, living or dead, is purely coincidental and not intended by the author.

All brand names and product names used in this book are trademarks, registered trademarks, or trade names of their respective holders. Wolfpack Publishing is not associated with any product or vendor in this book.

Edited by My Brother's Editor

Paperback ISBN 979-8-89567-753-7
Ebook ISBN 979-8-89567-752-0
LCCN 2025948118

BOOKED

For

CHRISTMAS

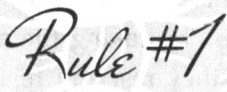

Rule #1

FAKE IT LIKE YOUR JOB DEPENDS ON IT

JULIA

THE KEYS JINGLE on my belt as I walk toward the perfectly polished glass front doors of The White Sands Resort. I could quiet them in my pocket, but I love the sound. It's the sound of power.

I was handed the official master key ring this afternoon when Sam, the general manager, entrusted me with being the last one out after making sure the generator technicians were finished, and all the alarms were set.

Not gonna lie, I was looking forward to my first big Christmas season at the resort on Faraday Island, where I have a feeling I'm soon going to be promoted to front desk manager. We'd been fully booked for the holiday for months by an investment firm in Minnesota. The staff spent the last month decorating and planning for a magical Christmas week.

A snowstorm that grounded all planes out of Minneapolis-Saint Paul took care of that.

The owners decided to take the whole staff on a cruise

as a holiday bonus—and give the hard-working resort generator time for a reset.

Someone had to stay behind and watch over the place, and I was the first to volunteer.

Not only do I live directly across the street from the resort, but I am endlessly dependable—and I'm about to prove it to the owners by taking the absolute best care of their property while they rest and rejuvenate for the busy second half of our season.

It's not like I have anyone to take with me on a cruise, anyway.

What I do have is a stack of books and a fridge filled with eggs, bread, and fruit. Not exactly the stuff Christmas movies are made of, but doing a great job at this will be a huge boost to my future promotability here at The White Sands.

I'm getting ready to slide the lock into place when I hear what sounds an awful lot like a roller suitcase being dragged up the bumpy concrete driveway.

But that's impossible.

Right?

I open the door quickly and step out, watching, to my shock and horror, as a frazzled-looking old woman in a wrinkled purple linen dress drags her dusty black hardshell roller bag up the sloped drive toward the front door. A cloud of dust rises up behind her, and I can just make out a golf cart, speeding away down the coral sand road.

The woman pauses when she sees me and lets go of the suitcase to put both hands on her hips as she tries to catch her breath.

The suitcase, of course, starts rolling backward down the driveway, toppling over halfway down and flopping end over end until it comes to rest in the sand with a thud.

I'm still staring at it, mouth hanging wide open, when

her frustrated shout snaps me out of my confused daze and back into customer service mode.

"A little help here?"

I spring into action. "Of course!"

Chasing the suitcase down, I drag it back up to stand next to the woman. On a normal day, I'd take it right into the lobby and set it on a rolling cart to be taken up to her room…but this is not a normal day.

I stand stupidly next to her in the blazing December sun and try my best to be polite. "Are you lost?"

It's the wrong thing to say, and the woman's narrowed glare lets me know that right away.

"Is this The White Sands Resort?"

"Yes…" I answer hesitantly.

"Then, no. I'm not lost."

She leaves me and her luggage standing on the pavement and marches the rest of the way up the drive and into the lobby. I have no choice but to follow her.

"Your A/C sucks," she tells me as I drag her suitcase through the front door.

"Well, it's—"

"I should have an ocean view suite reserved. The name is Margo Vale."

That shuts me up.

I may be a lowly hotel clerk from po-dunk Oregon who only got left in charge of this resort out of sheer necessity, but even I know the name Margo Vale.

She's *The New York Times* hospitality columnist who once made an infamous French chef cry.

"Yes, of course, Mrs. Vale—"

"Ms.," she corrects me with her sharp tongue.

"Ms. Vale." I try to recover, smoothing my hair down and thanking the gods I showed up to the resort today in my full uniform—rather than take a "casual day" in jean shorts and tank tops like other staff members might have. "Let me just pull that reservation up."

Behind the front desk, the sunlight coming in from the windows barely lights the keyboard—not that it would do me much good. With the main generator down for at least a day for its firmware update, the resort has zero power.

I tap away at the keys anyway, trying to look busily at my dark screen while sneaking my cell phone out of my pocket. Reception is spotty on a good day, but it's been known to come through here and there.

This is not one of those days.

> Sam- this is Julia. We have an unexpected important guest who didn't get the memo about the holiday being canceled. What should I do?

It fails to send.

Praying it's just his phone and not mine, I try three more texts to the other three owners, even though I know damn well they're on a boat somewhere, headed out to sea for their much-deserved holiday cruise.

Fail, fail, fail.

"How long does it take to look up a reservation?" the woman demands, leaning over the counter as if she's trying to see the screen.

Joke's on her. There's not a damn thing on this screen.

"Sorry, Ms. Vale. I was just trying to make sure..."

I tap a few more times to buy myself some time to think.

What I should do is tell this woman the truth. That the resort is closed for maintenance, and all the staff are on a cruise.

But I know there's not a snowball's chance in hell of finding this woman somewhere else to stay. Unless I plan to give her my own bed, she's going to be sleeping in a beach hammock.

And then there's her job—and her reputation.

I heard one harrowing story from a bartender about this woman getting a bed-and-breakfast in Nantucket shuttered after finding a blueberry stem in her yogurt parfait.

I've only had this job for a season, and it's the best shot I have at making an actual career for myself. The last thing I need is for this place to get shut down because one grumpy old lady didn't get her oceanfront suite.

My mind goes through its usual solution listing exercise, trying to find the perfect plan to handle this.

I could settle this woman in a chair with a cool drink and head straight to town, hoping to catch the cruise ship before it sets sail.

I could head to my house and use my landline to call the emergency number the owners left me, the caretakers of their property on Merit Island.

But how would it reflect on me if I needed help the second an issue came up?

They trusted me with this job because they knew I was responsible, resourceful, and I could handle it. I will not be proving them wrong one hour into my duties. Everyone has been working hard these last few months, with the resort busier than ever, and they all deserve this long weekend to relax. I can't even begin to imagine the shame of having to look everyone in the eyes as they trudged back to work on Christmas Eve eve to take care of one silly woman whom I couldn't manage on my own.

"The reservation could be under my brother's name," Margo barks, interrupting my heroic decision-making process. "Harry Blund. He's a lawyer in Minnesota. It was his company that planned this whole shit show of a vacation."

That explains things. She must not have heard that the entire rest of her party is stuck in a snowbank in the Midwest.

"Have you talked to your brother recently?" I ask, trying to sound like I'm making polite conversation.

The woman just huffs. "Phones don't work for crap around here. I flew in from Mexico. I was there for a month on some newfangled 'yoga for seniors' retreat I got roped into. What a mess."

And that explains why she was able to arrive here while everyone else got stranded.

I just hope the owners and the entire staff understand what an enormous favor I'm doing them.

"Well, Ms. Vale, I'm sorry to have to let you know your brother and his work associates weren't able to make it out of the States. There was a blizzard that grounded all planes in the region."

She waves her hand at me dismissively. "I'm sure they'll be here tomorrow. That sort of thing happens all the time."

I plaster on my best customer service smile. "Of course. Well, let me show you to your room."

Everyone knows the very best suites are in the penthouses at the top of the resort. But considering the power is out and I have no idea when or if it will come back on, the first floor is all I have to work with. I'm certain this grumpy old lady isn't going to react well to walking up and down eight flights of stairs.

I wheel her suitcase down the long first-floor hallway toward a very nice room with a patio that opens right onto the beach. It's close to the lobby and pool area and is often used as the bridal suite for resort weddings.

This time of day, the sun is at just the right angle to almost make it seem like the lights are on...but it's only a matter of time before my guest realizes the truth. I decide to get out ahead of that.

As she's strolling around the massive one-bedroom suite, opening and closing drawers, running her finger over the white windowsills, and checking the shower pressure, I clear my throat.

She turns like she's forgotten I exist.

"The generator went offline this morning for scheduled maintenance, and we're still waiting for it to reset."

Her eyebrows nearly disappear between her helmet of lavender-gray curls. "Ah. So, your A/C doesn't suck. There's just no power."

I nod, relieved that she seems to be taking it so well.

That feeling is short-lived.

"That's much worse. How am I supposed to see in the dark?"

I'm a smiling, nodding, customer service robot. "I'll be filling your suite with battery-powered lights and candles."

"And the hot water?"

"We should have enough in the tank to last for a while, but many of our guests find a cool shower very refreshing."

I almost amuse her with that answer.

Almost.

"And how are you planning to make my Gin Rickeys without any ice?"

That is an excellent question.

I know damn well my face doesn't falter, and yet she seems to know she got me. The woman must be able to smell my fear.

"Not a problem, Ms. Vale. Our kitchen is on a separate generator."

It's a lie, but it's officially time for me to get the heck out of this room—and down to said kitchen to shovel as much ice out of the rapidly warming ice machine into the rapidly warming walk-in freezer as I can before, well, before this whole charade becomes a lukewarm puddle.

"Well, if it gets too unbearable in here, I might need to move into that kitchen."

It's more of a threat than a joke, but I laugh lightheartedly as I back toward the door. "I'm just going to head to the bar and get you a drink, okay Ms. Vale? If you need anything, just...well...um...just have a seat on the patio and enjoy the lovely ocean breeze. I'll be back in ten minutes."

She's saying something as I close the door behind me, but there's no time to wait.

Rule #2

BEWARE OF COLD STORAGE

JULIA

I SPRINT down the hallway as quickly as I can in more or less pitch darkness, saving my phone battery for my imminent cocktail rescue mission.

The kitchen is even warmer than the lobby, with no windows to offer fresh air. I pull off my uniform blazer and strap my long hair into a ponytail. Ready.

Propping my phone up on the central prep table and locating a tub large enough for three days' worth of ice, I set to work shoveling it full and then drag it over to the doors of the walk-in cooler.

I haven't spent a lot of time in this kitchen, but I know my way around well enough to maneuver in the low light. And I've been an adult long enough to know that there isn't really anything lurking in the dark waiting to attack, no matter what our lingering childhood fears might be telling us.

I grab my phone and hold it ahead of me as I pull the door open…

Only to have my worst nightmare come true.

"Can I help you?" the man inside the cooler asks.

I scream and back up so quickly I trip over something and fall flat on my ass, still shuffling backward to try and flee from the intruder.

The shirtless intruder.

Who is not exactly chasing me.

I scramble to my feet and snatch my phone from the floor where I dropped it, shining the light ahead of me.

Even with his hand raised to shield his eyes from the blinding phone flashlight, I recognize him. It's Wes, one of the Raft sous chefs.

"What are you doing here?" I hiss. "And why aren't you dressed?"

He just tosses me that cocky smile I'm used to seeing on his lips as the girls on staff drool over him. "I could ask you the same question."

I look down at my fully clothed body, aghast. "I'm dressed."

Wes steps out of the cooler and closes the door behind him. It's only then I notice that his hair is wet. And his feet are bare. "That you are, Mary Poppins. But it doesn't explain why you're here."

"I'm closing up the resort for the holiday," I start, unsure how much I want to share. I mean, how would I even explain myself? A guest showed up, so I gave her a room even though there's no staff or power?

It sounds insane.

It is insane.

"Kitchen's taken care of," he responds, arms folded across his bare chest.

Which reminds me...

"If you're here working, why aren't you wearing a shirt? Or shoes?"

As I glare down at his toes, I spot the large, dark lump that tripped me a second ago.

It's a duffel bag.

And a pillow.

"Wes, what the hell?"

He crosses the kitchen toward me, hands held up in surrender. "It's not what it looks like."

I back away until I'm up against the wall. "It looks like you're planning to sleep here."

"Dom asked me to watch over the kitchen during the closure. To make sure the pilots all stay lit and no one,"—he takes a step closer, raising his eyebrows at me—"sneaks in to steal anything."

It does sound possible, but...

"Sam left me in charge of locking up and watching over the place," I reply. "I would have been told if you were staying behind as well."

He shrugs. "You know how Dom is. He likes to do his own thing."

I do know how Chef Dominic is. Stern, secretive, and fiercely protective of his restaurants.

But if he was going to leave his own security, would he really have chosen this guy?

Don't get me wrong. Wes is known for his culinary talent. He has the magic touch when it comes to soups and sauces. But he's also known for being a bit of a rogue. More than once, I've heard the front desk staff talk about how he's being disciplined again for being late, or for his uniform not being up to the standards required for the dining room presentations all chefs do during the tasting menu dinner service. He's undeniably charismatic, which is probably why he's made it this long, but he just isn't well suited to the Pendleton-badged level of Raft.

"I'll just call to make sure," I lie, holding my phone up to light the screen as if it had a drop of reception.

My bluff works.

"Hold on," Wes says, stepping even closer.

I can't back away any further with my back against the wall, and I'm suddenly very aware of my situation—trapped in the dark basement kitchen of an empty resort with a man whose livelihood I just threatened.

I take a deep breath and prepare to go on the offensive—rushing forward in a surprise attack and knocking him flat on his ass before I run for my life—when he backs up.

"You got me, okay?"

I narrow my eyes as he backs up further.

"I've been camping out down here for a few months. It won't be forever, but—"

"You're living down here?" I'm appalled, and the question comes out as more of a shriek.

Wes flinches. "Calm down there, Poppins. It's not that big of a deal."

I beg to differ. "It's a huge deal to be squatting in a commercial kitchen. It's completely unhygienic for one thing—"

"I'm not living in the kitchen. That would be impossible. I'm just…there's a small storage closet down near the water heaters that no one uses anymore, and I set up camp there."

"Don't you have an apartment in staff housing?"

I know the answer is yes because I went to a small party there my first week on the island, before I knew better.

His one-bedroom apartment was a regular bachelor pad flop house, and it incensed me that someone would take such a blessing for granted. I, myself, have been living in a tiny, two-room shack of a cabin in someone's side yard for months waiting for an apartment in staff housing to open up.

"I...I did."

"What do you mean you did?"

He opens his mouth to offer some ridiculous story that I'm not going to believe anyway, so I don't bother waiting. "Never mind. I don't care. I don't have time for this."

His infuriatingly handsome face cracks into an equally infuriatingly handsome smile. "Oh? And what are you in such a rush to do? Get home to your cat?"

An unexpected bubble of emotion swells in my gut when I consider my answer.

I don't even have a cat to go home to.

It's then I decide.

While I don't need any help pulling off my superhero mission of giving the entire resort staff the fun-filled vacation they deserve—while also saving our asses from a terrible review in the Times, I can't deny that the whole thing would be easier with someone to cook while I did literally everything else that goes into running a resort for our one guest.

"There's someone here."

"What do you mean?"

I shrug. "A guest of a guest who didn't get the memo that the whole party was canceled and the resort shut down."

He scoffs. "You need me to kick her to the curb?"

"It's Margo Vale."

It's clear by his twisted grimace that he knows exactly who that is. "Really?"

I nod.

"What are you going to do?"

"What are *we* going to do?" I raise my hand to halt any objections Wes is clearly preparing to offer at his inclusion. "I already tried to get in contact with the owners. There's no reception. Everyone's gone on the cruise. This lady could destroy the entire resort with one review, and we are the ones who have been left in charge of the resort. It's up to us to save it."

"Okay, okay. It's going to be alright." Wes's whole tone changes, and I'm able to take a deep breath for the first time since that lady showed up at our front door.

He doesn't want to, but he's going to stay. He's going to help me.

"Aren't there caretakers—"

"I'm not calling them." I put my foot down.

Wes's face twists with confusion. "Why not?"

"Because we don't need them. It's one freaking guest. And besides, do you really want to be the one to ruin someone's Christmas by dragging them over here to clean up a mess we are perfectly capable of containing ourselves?"

He doesn't look convinced, so I plow forward. "All we need is to make it three days, then everyone will be back."

"They'll be back and wondering why the hell we didn't call them."

"Or," I start, digging deep to appeal to what I think will motivate him. "They'll be so grateful and well-rested that they promote us both."

This fails. "You're assuming everyone wants to be promoted."

I scoff. "Everyone does want to be promoted." Why wouldn't they?

"How about this?" he starts, "I'll take the golf cart up the hill to—"

"Are you crazy? You're not leaving me here!"

Not ten minutes ago, I was ready and willing to do this alone. Now that I've had help dangled in front of me, I'm not about to give it up.

"I'll come back—"

"Like hell you will."

He doesn't argue, and I congratulate myself silently for seeing right through his plan.

He's still sneaking glances at the door, however, as if calculating when to make a run for it.

"I'll tell," I announce.

That gets his attention. The full weight of his crystal blue-eyed gaze settles on mine in the dim light of my phone. "You wouldn't."

He's probably right, but I can't let him know that.

"I would. I will. If you don't stay here and help me, I'll tell Sam and Dominic the second I see them that you've been squatting in the basement."

Wes grinds his teeth and sucks in a long breath through his nose.

The suspense of the moment nearly kills me.

Finally, he just shakes his head. "What do you want me to do?"

My mouth drops open. "I..."

His brow crinkles adorably, and I consider pretending my phone battery died just so we can have this conversation in the dark. This man might be a total screwup professionally, but there's a reason all the girls whisper about him behind his back.

He's the ultimate bad-boy heartthrob archetype, with hair just long enough to fall over one eye, piercing blue irises, and strong, tan arms covered in tattoos. Standing in front of me now, shirtless, water dripping from the ends of his dark curls, my mind tries to spin me a scenario where he just stepped out of my shower, wrapped in a towel...

As if a man who looks like this would ever be in my shower.

As if a man who looks like this would ever take a second glance at an uncool, uptight, rule follower like me.

Hell, as if I'd ever *want* a guy like this around. Imagine

being seen with him around the resort. That could spell ruin for my own, carefully planned career advancement.

"C'mon. Lay it out for me," Wes says, leaning on the stainless-steel prep table.

I take a deep breath, shaking off any remaining thoughts of him in a towel, in my house, and tell him everything I know. "You already know who she is, so you know why I didn't just send her packing."

He nods.

"I guess her brother is one of the lawyers at the investment firm, and he invited her for Christmas. She was already in Mexico when the snowstorm hit, and he couldn't get a hold of her to tell her the reservation was off. And now she's here. She's ornery as hell and displeased that the A/C doesn't work, and she drinks Gin Rickeys."

"Well," he answers casually, reaching into the black duffel to pull out a soft-looking, sky-blue tee, muscles flexing tight over his stomach and chest as he reaches up to pull the shirt over his head. "That's as good a place as any to start."

Wes looks just as handsome and confident behind the bar as he always does in his chef whites.

"Gin Rickey sounds like an old-person drink, but it's actually pretty simple," he tells me, filling a tall, narrow glass with ice from a tub we brought up here.

He agreed that getting as much as we could into the freezer was a great idea—obviously—and assured me that it would stay cool enough in there to keep the ice frozen for three days.

"Two ounces of Tanqueray, half a squeezed lime," he talks me through it.

I'm engrossed.

In a purely professional way, of course. I am going to have to make this drink myself soon enough, after all.

"Top with club soda," he says, cracking the top of a tiny can.

I take note of how slowly he pours the soda, deftly avoiding it fizzing up, while his large, tan hand holds the glass in place. My gaze has just started to creep up his golden brown, tattooed forearms when he shocks me back to attention by shoving a long, silver spoon into the glass.

"One quick stir should do it."

He adds a half-moon slice of lime and slides the drink across the bar.

It's all I can do not to dive headfirst into the refreshing-looking drink to cool myself off.

Wes must see me drooling, because when I look up, he's giving me a sideways grin. "Deliver that one to the old lady, and I'll make you one of your own, Poppins."

Relief pours over me when he incorrectly thinks I'm all hot and bothered over the cocktail. "Why do you call me that?"

He shrugs. "Blue skirt, starched white blouse, too-tight bun. Perfect red lipstick. Always look like you're about to scold me. I call it how I see it."

"Careful, cowboy. Your childhood trauma is showing." I pull off the perfect turn and exit, and just in time because I know my cheeks are flushed from delivering that inappropriate and completely out of character sassy comeback. I don't know what's gotten into me.

Wes follows me to the suite, even though I do not invite him.

I expect to find Margo changed into something comfortable, relaxing on her gorgeous deck in the cool ocean breeze, but she's sitting more or less exactly where I left her, in the chair by the bed, wearing her dusty travel clothes. Looking less than pleased.

"I made you a Gin Rickey, Ms. Vale."

Wes clears his throat from the doorway in protest, and I toss a glare at him as I cross the room and place the dripping glass in our guest's outstretched hand.

"Thank you," she says simply, falling on the cocktail like a life raft.

I can't help but notice most of the fight has gone out of her. "Are you okay?" I ask.

"I will be in about five minutes," she snipes back.

Honestly, I'm almost relieved. I'm not sure what I'd do if she fell over dead or something.

"Who's that?" she asks sharply, gesturing with her chin to where Wes still leans in the doorway.

I glance back at him before beaming my brightest smile at Margo. "Wes..." I realize too late I have no idea what his last name is. "Is going to be your chef for the holiday," I recover quickly.

Margo looks less than convinced. "Why does he look like you just dragged him out of your bed?"

I hear Wes snort behind me and look back just in time to see him toss a playful wink at Margo. When I whip my head back around, she's smiling conspiratorially.

"I did nothing of the sort. I do apologize for his unprofessional attire, but rest assured he will be in uniform next time you see him."

I march over to the door and shove Wes into the hallway, turning back to Margo with a smile. "We're just getting the dining room ready for you. I'll come to collect you in about an hour for dinner. Will that be okay?"

"Have another one of these sent up in the meantime," the old lady answers, holding up her cocktail.

I close the door and chase Wes down the hallway, ready to read him the riot act.

But he's gone.

Rule #3

MIX COCKTAILS, NOT FEELINGS

WES

I NOW KNOW how the Grinch felt when the townspeople showed up and ruined his quiet, peaceful Christmas alone in his cave.

I had the perfect week planned.

The pool and hot tub all to myself.

Old movies on the big screen in the theater room.

Sleeping in one of the hammocks on the patio, swaying in the ocean breeze.

I even splurged on decadent groceries to cook all my favorite meals. It was hardly something I could afford, but it is Christmas after all. I'll make it up in January. I hope.

But now?

The whole thing's a wash.

I'm going to spend the week cooking my steaks for some newspaper critic in hopes of her not noticing this whole thing is one big damn charade.

Trouble finds me before I'm ready.

"There you are," Julia calls out as she comes around the

corner into the bar area of the grand room in the main lobby. The room has three-story high ceilings with windows covering the entire ocean facing wall, and an unnecessary fireplace that gets lit only a few times a year—for purely decorative purposes.

It was this room I was most looking forward to having to myself this week.

I've always wanted to watch the stars come out through those windows. To watch a rainstorm roll in over the ocean and overtake the blue skies.

"Here I am," I answer, not looking up from where I'm mixing three more Gin Rickeys.

Jules flops onto the stool across from where I stand and rests her head on her folded arms.

She's looking more ruffled and unkempt than I've ever seen her before. A hint of dark smudge under her eye where the heat got the best of her mascara. Wisps of sandy hair escaping from her customary ponytail creating a bit of a halo around her head.

Disheveled looks good on her.

This woman has been buttoned up to level one hundred since the day she set foot on this property. I've never seen her without her mask of perfection painted on. From her always pressed white blouses to the black pumps she must actually polish, she's got *something to prove* written all over her.

What is it about a perfectly wrapped package that makes me want to tear it open so badly?

Not that she'd ever deign to lower herself to the likes of me.

A girl like this has places to go, and I know for a fact she's not interested in risking her position as queen of the front desk for a detour to the hotel basement.

In another life, maybe she and I could have seen eye-to-eye.

But all we have is this life right now, and in this life? I've got goals of my own. And I don't care what people think of me, not even this sexy librarian, as long as I'm able to reach them.

"Three more of those will probably put that lady in the ground, Wes."

I shake my head because she's dead wrong. I saw that old lady suck down her cocktail. She's had some practice. "Might put her to bed, sure. But then we'd have the night off."

Jules tightens her pretty face back into a stern pout, and I can't help but smile. "I'm joking. This one's for me." I take a long pull, watching Julia's eyes follow the black straw between my lips. "Not half bad."

She bites her own lip and blinks as if trying to wipe something out of her mind.

I wonder if I'm ever going to find out what it is.

"What," she starts, her voice cracking just a bit. She clears her throat and flushes the most adorable shade of pink.

"What about those two?" she asks, recovering her confident tone, but unable to hide the blush.

"This one," I hold one of the cocktails up and hold back a smile as she almost reaches for it but restrains herself. "Is for our guest, of course."

Her gaze narrows as she homes in on the third glass. "And that one?"

"That one," I tell her, setting down Margo's drink and lifting the final glass. "Was just the tester. I'm going to pour it out—"

Julia leans over the bar and snatches it out of my hand,

flopping back down on her stool and sucking down half of the drink in one long pull.

I laugh and shake my head. "Take it easy. We've got a long night ahead of us."

She rolls her eyes and sets the glass down but doesn't release her grip on it. "A long night of pretending to be a welcoming five-star resort when we're actually just an abandoned building on the beach."

Taking a sip of my own drink, I cock my head at her. "What's the plan exactly?"

She glances around the massive room, decorated in its standard high-end beach resort casual, and sighs. "We've gotta get just enough decor up in here to make it look intentional. We're never going to pull off the makeover."

She's not wrong there.

This room had been decked to the rafters with holiday glitz and glamour before the big, all-staff take-down party the day before. The owners wanted a clean slate going into the new year when everyone returned from the cruise.

We had this place cleaned up in just a few short hours, but I remember all too well the full week it took to put all that crap up. It would be impossible for the two of us to recreate that level of splendor in just under an hour.

I nod, considering. It'll be simple enough to throw some lights up and swap out the decorative pillows. I know there's a fully decorated fake palm tree hiding downstairs because I dragged the damn thing down there myself. "And the plan for the rest of the week? This place isn't exactly stocked for guests. I'm sure she'll be happy to lie out on the beach for a while, but it seems to me that Christmas guests generally come expecting, well, Christmas."

Jules twirls her straw between her ruby red lips and for a hot minute, I forget all about our current predicament.

"Well, you're the only one who can wear the Santa suit, so..."

I nearly choke on my swallow of gin as the hall monitor herself makes a joke. "Dang, Poppins. Never would have guessed you had a Saint Nick kink."

Her eyes go wide as saucers and her cheeks flush. "That's not what I meant. I was just..." Her embarrassment shifts swiftly to annoyance. "Never mind."

She's on her feet and moving toward the window, pretending to examine the sheer drapes—but I know avoidance when I see it. Pounding the rest of my cocktail, I follow her.

"What about food? I don't suppose you're going to let me run to town to stock up on eggs and bread."

She spins to face me, and her mask of perfect calm is back in place. "I have eggs and bread," she replies quickly. "I actually got a bunch of groceries. I was planning to spend the whole week at my house, just in case I had to run across the street if the resort needed anything."

Now that's something I have a hard time slotting into my preconceived notions of exactly what this woman is about. "No family to go home to? No rich lawyer boyfriend to make cookies for?"

She turns back to the window, but not before I catch a crack in her calm mask.

"I..." she starts.

And I'll be damned if I'm not sorry I said anything. "I got a bunch of groceries as well," I say quickly. "Good stuff. Steaks and cheese and wine. The full works. It's in a cooler in the walk-in. I planned to spend the holiday prowling around the empty resort."

"Great," she answers, still not turning around.

I'm just reaching up to put a comforting hand on her shoulder and apologize for being a dick when she marches off toward the hallway leading to the service stairs.

She's talking as she goes, so I have no choice but to follow.

"Between your food and my food, we'll have to just make it work."

She spins at the top of the stairwell and faces me, her eyes narrowed in an appraising glare. "You can make that work, can't you? Pull off three meals a day without a fully stocked walk-in and chef to create menus?"

I try not to take her dig personally…and fail. "Of course. I'm more than just a line cook, you know."

Jules does not look convinced, but what choice does she have? She did blackmail me in to helping. She's stuck with me.

"Clock's ticking, boss," I jab, raising my eyebrows impatiently, as if I just can't wait to start decorating.

Jules narrows her eyes once more as if she's going to tell me off, but then she just rolls them and continues down the stairs.

With my intimate knowledge of the resort's basement storage closets, I'm able to lead us straight to the holiday decor section. Julia drags over a wooden ladder and prepares to climb, her gaze locked on a large, cardboard box labeled White Twinkle Lights.

"You sure you're good to climb up there?"

She scoffs down at me from the third rung, preparing to deliver some witty comeback, I'm sure, but the motion of her turning shakes the ladder enough that she has to reverse course and wrap both arms around it to keep from falling.

"I'll hold it steady, captain," I offer, gripping the wooden rails.

She seems to relax and resumes her climb up to the top,

passing the lights box down in a precarious operation that, luckily, goes off without a hitch.

Confidence boosted, she climbs to the tippy top of the ladder, dragging another box down from the shelf and pulling the flaps open to peer inside.

"Searching for elves?" I joke up at her.

As if she somehow forgot I was down there, Julia turns her head to glare down at me. "Are you looking up my skirt?"

I honestly hadn't even thought of that, my full concentration on my task of catching her if she was to topple off the ladder.

"No, ma'am," I answer, shaking my head.

She's unconvinced. "Close your eyes."

This is not the smartest move, but the last thing I want is for her to think I'm trying to sneak a peek under her tight, thigh-length navy-blue skirt. I mean, what could possibly be under there? Is she hiding some fancy lace undies? Or no undies at all?

I squeeze my eyes tightly closed, knowing damn well they're going to wander up that skirt now if left to their own devices. "Blind as a bat."

"Are you sure you're not peeking?"

"I'm sure," I report, gripping the wooden ladder in complete darkness.

I can feel her start to shift on the ladder. I hear a box sliding on the shelf above.

But I'm in no way prepared for that box to come crashing down on my head.

"Hey!" I cry, stumbling backward, eyes flying open just in time to see the box slide forward off my head and land on the lower rungs of the ladder.

Sending the thing toppling sideways.

I react just in time, lurching forward, stumbling over the

box of lights, and catching Julia before she lands on her knees on the concrete floor.

"What are you doing?" I demand, righting myself and settling her onto unsteady feet.

"I thought you were peeking," she answers breathlessly.

"Hell of a way to check, Julia. You could've landed on your head."

"You...you know my name," she answers, blinking at me like she doesn't know who I am.

"Of course, I know your name. Everyone knows your name." I just mean because we're coworkers in a small resort on a small island. Everyone knows everyone.

I'm not sure that's how she takes it, though. It's pretty dim in here, but I'm sure I see walls slam down behind her eyes.

Maybe she did hit her head after all.

"Sit down," I tell her, taking her shoulders and stepping her over to sit on the cardboard box.

She obeys, even though she looks like she'd rather tell me to piss off.

Just as the box takes her weight, the tape gives, and she falls through.

An ill-timed laugh escapes my lips, and I try to shut it down, but it's too late.

Julia shoves off my attempt to help her up and struggles until the box topples on its side, and she rolls out onto the floor.

I manage to grab her wrists and pull her up, but she stumbles toward me, wrists still held tightly in my hands, until her chest meets mine.

The moment lingers longer than I expect it to, her ribcage rising and falling quickly as she catches her breath. Our bodies pressed together in the rapidly warming dark.

Must be the lack of A/C...

Julia seems to come to all at once, taking an unsteady step backward and jerking out of my grasp. Our eyes meet, and I can just make out a wide-eyed flash of...something... before she looks away.

And snaps straight back into work mode. "Come on. We don't have time for this."

Grabbing the box of lights, she takes off through the open door of the storage room.

I lift the other box under my arm and follow, snagging the fake palm tree from a corner and dragging it along behind me.

Rule #4

NO BODY, NO CRIME

WES

GOLDEN HOUR in the grand room of the resort is brilliant on a normal day. Today? It's like the gods are smiling down on us with dazzling rays of sunshine, cutting through the palms at just the right angle to light up the festively decorated palm tree I set up in the corner.

Which is lucky, considering dusk is rapidly approaching, and we've had no indication that the generator is going to join the party.

Julia keeps assuring Margo that we're just waiting for it to "reset," which should happen "at any time"...but I'm starting to suspect she has no idea when—or if—it's ever coming back on at all.

Our barely pacified guest dines by herself on the patio with a green tablecloth blowing gently in the ocean breeze. A tall, red candle in a hurricane glass lights up the space, and a Jimmy Buffett Christmas album—that Jules apparently already had downloaded—plays on a Bluetooth speaker hidden in a planter.

So, you know, holiday magic.

It was tragic to watch one of the ribeye steaks I hand-selected from the butcher for my own dinner carried out to the old lady's table, but I'll get over it, thanks in no small part to the Gin Rickeys still flowing.

Good Girl Julia, in all of her rule-following glory, seems to have no issue with her and I sharing in the spoils of the unlocked liquor cabinet. I guess she thinks we deserve it, considering we're going out of our way to keep this damn resort alive. And I must say, I agree.

"She looks so lonely out there," Julia murmurs, leaning on the bar across from me as we try not to get caught watching Margo eat dinner.

"Pssht," I huff in reply. "Dinner alone is one of life's great pleasures."

The look Julia shoots me is a cross between disgust and pity, but I shake it off. I'm right, and I know it. Sure, sharing meals with people can be enjoyable, but nothing beats being left the hell alone.

Hence, my plans for the holiday.

And now that I think about it, Julia's.

"Weren't you planning to eat eggs and toast alone in your house all week?" I ask.

She tosses me some side-eye. "Yeah. But I need to watch over the resort."

"Ah," I answer, giving the gleaming wooden bar top a completely unnecessary wipe. "So, if you didn't need to be here, you'd have flown home for a cozy family Christmas, complete with snow and eggnog?"

She says nothing, pretending to be busy watching our guest.

"Or taken a Mediterranean holiday with your lover?"

She rolls her eyes at me. "Why do you care?"

I shrug. "I don't really. Just making—"

"Conversation?" she interrupts, turning on me. "Don't bother. I'm busy working. Why don't you go make conv—"

She cuts herself off and bites her lip.

My smile is wide and smug. "Go make conversation with someone else, Poppins? Is that what you were going to suggest? I can't do that because everyone else is gone. And I can't even sit silently out on that deck," I point to where Margo is sipping red wine, "and enjoy my perfectly cooked steak in peace because you told that guest she could stay and blackmailed me into helping you. So, yes, I do plan on talking to you for the next three days because you're the only person here."

Jules calls my bluff perfectly by walking away without answering.

Margo turns down dessert, which is just as well, considering how hard it would be to convince her that my Phish Food ice cream was house-made. I take her a glass of sherry, which lights up her entire face in the most pleasant expression I've seen from her so far.

She and I may get along after all.

"I don't want to spoil it for you," I tease, "but none of them make it off the island alive."

Margo sets down her battered copy of *And Then There Were None* and narrows her eyes at me. "I thought your generation only read on your phones."

I shrug. "My mom was a big reader. All the shelves in my house growing up were lined with paperback mysteries. I think she had that very copy." I gesture to the cover, which has to be twenty years old.

Margo sips her sherry and nods. "It's one of my all-time favorites. I read it over and over. New books just disappoint."

"Good thing you're not a book critic, eh?"

I mean it as a lighthearted joke, but the shadow that

passes over the old woman's expression lets me know I hit a bit too close to home.

"Literary work would have been my first choice."

"But..." I lead shamelessly.

"But we don't always get what we want in life," she replies shortly, retreating from the casual exchange. "Surely you've figured that out by now."

"Yes, ma'am," I answer before I can stop myself.

When she cocks her head curiously, as if she's about to begin an inquisition into my life's failures, I retreat to the safety of the bar.

I'm polishing glasses when Jules returns with the empty sherry glass. "Margo's going to turn in early. She says she's exhausted from the trip."

"Great," I reply, unsure of how much I care about any of this.

"And she wants to get up early and go snorkeling."

I snort before I can catch myself. "I'm not taking her snorkeling."

"Yes," Jules hisses, leaning over the bar, "we are."

I shake my head. "Snorkel guides are snorkel guides for a reason. They're trained to save people in the ocean."

Julia has no patience for this. She actually kind of looks like she's about to punch me. "It'll be fine, wimp. I went with a group to a cove nearby where you snorkel right from the beach. We'll take her in the small boat. I'm sure I can drive it."

I'm not sure about any of this, but I can see there's no talking her out of it. "Okay, but we need to make a pact right now. If she dies out there, we just sink her body down to the bottom for the fish to eat and never tell anyone she was here."

I could not have surprised Julia more if I slapped her across the face.

She does not, however, argue with me. "I'm going to run to my house to get the breakfast stuff."

"The hell you are. You're not leaving me alone here."

"It's fine, Wes. If worst comes to worst, you can just kill her and put her body in the furnace."

"I'll need your help chopping her up small enough to fit through the grate."

"Oh my god, you fucking psychopath! I can't even with this. I'm going to my house."

"Great. I'll grab my hat."

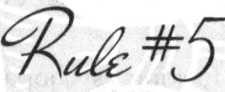

Rule #5

KEEP YOUR TROPES TO YOURSELF

JULIA

I SPEND the three-minute walk from the resort drowning in nervous anxiety about the state of my house.

Did I pick my dirty laundry up off the floor?

Did I hide my little pink vibrator?

Will he laugh at my childhood stocking, strung up over a makeshift pile of sticks and handcrafted paper fire I made to try and infuse the tiniest bit of my childhood traditions into this lonely year?

My hands shake as I unlock the door.

"This place is great, Julia," Wes says from behind me.

I turn as I open the door and find him spinning in place on the small, concrete stoop, taking in the well-groomed jungle garden my landlords have been tending for the last fifty years.

"It's very small," I reply, stepping inside and leaving the door open, as I'm sure he won't put up with being left outside.

My laundry is on the bed, but at least the bed is made.

No vibrators in sight.

Now I've just gotta grab what I need and get us the hell out of here before—

"Well, well, well," Wes clicks his tongue behind me.

I already know what he found, so I don't bother turning around. I just keep shoving groceries into my two insulated totes, pretending I don't care at all that he's now pawing through my deepest, darkest secrets.

"I've actually read some of these, you know."

It's probably a trick, but I fall for it.

"You have not." I spit the words, spinning around to glare at him.

The book he's holding in his hand right now makes my heart drop to my stomach.

I don't even really like that particular book, with its *"shamefully recessive portrayal of marriage and feminism and idolization of the hyper-alpha male archetype,"* as several FanReads reviewers commented.

By which I mean I didn't know I would like it, until I read it. And now it's my most re-read book, the pages heavy with highlights and annotations. I own four different special edition copies.

"What the actual fuck—" Wes cracks it open to somewhere in the center. I can see line after line highlighted in pink—and I know exactly what that means.

Crossing the room in one giant leap, I snatch the book out of his hands. "It was here when I moved in," I tell him, the lie so painfully obvious, he doesn't even bother to point it out.

"You're hiding a little freak behind that buttoned-up blouse, is that it, Poppins?"

"No," I reply, but it comes out as a whisper as I focus on the floor around my feet.

"Oh, okay." He takes a step closer, but I'm frozen to the

spot. "So that wasn't you in your bed with the pink high-lighter, imagining some strange man breaking into your house and taking you by force?"

"He's not a stranger," I manage to squeak out.

Wes takes another step closer. He's warm and smells like man, and he's right up in my personal space. "What was that?"

"He's her stalker," I reply a bit louder. "Not a stranger."

I dare a glance up and meet Wes's gaze. I'm expecting to see humor there, as he prepares to make fun of me.

But that's not at all what I find shining in his deep blue eyes.

"Is that right?" he murmurs, low and rough, just like he would if he was the guy from one of my books.

"I think we should probably get back..." I tell him, trying to sound confident but failing miserably.

Wes just shakes his head, distracting me with his dazzling blue eyes as he grabs the book back. "There was something else I saw in here." He flips until he comes to a solid block of green highlighter.

Oh gods.

"Something about a necklace..." He clicks his tongue as he scans the page.

I should take the book back.

I should run.

I should do anything but stand here, waiting for him to find what I know he's going to find.

But, of course, I don't.

"Ah, yes." He taps his finger against the page and nods.

Then tosses the book aside and takes another step toward me. "I've never admitted to anyone how often I fantasize about this myself..."

I take a small step back as he gets closer.

"I like knowing that you're thinking about it, too."

I take two steps back as he continues to stalk toward me.

"Do you trust me?" he asks in what could only be described as a growl.

I shake my head, and he smiles.

Freaking smiles.

"Are you lying?"

I blink several times, paralyzed by indecision.

Luckily—or unluckily—Wes continues to take the lead. "If you want me to stop, tell me to stop, got it?"

I manage to nod, though I'm starting to feel lightheaded. I can't remember the last time I took a breath. I suck one in to keep from dying, and it's louder than I intend. More like a gasp.

Wes smiles again and marches toward me, faster this time.

I back up until there's nowhere left to go, my back pressed into the wall.

He's right up against me, hips pressing my hips. I can feel his hardness through his jeans and all I can think is how wild it is that he's as turned on by a book as I am...

He reaches out to unbutton the collar of my blouse, and it's all I can do to hold still. Not to shift my weight and squeeze my thighs together. Not to let him know just how much this little scenario is doing it for me.

He opens the top three buttons and touches his fingers down on my bare collarbone. "Take a breath, Poppins."

I obey, sucking in a long, mercifully quiet one this time.

My heart is pounding so hard, it's all I can hear as he slides his hand up until he's got his long, strong fingers wrapped around my neck.

I've imagined this feeling so many times, book in one hand, vibrator in the other.

How confined I would feel.

How dangerous it would be.

But nothing my imagination came up with could ever match the feeling of what's happening right now.

Wes doesn't tighten his grip as much as he presses me harder into the wall, lifting up so my neck straightens. It's dominating and terrifying and so, so sexy.

I want to beg him to stop, but I'm too afraid that if I do, he will.

"Wes," I whisper, my voice coming out sounding so desperate. Needy.

He bares his teeth at me as his blue eyes darken. "What comes next, Poppins?"

I blink, unwilling to speak the words aloud. Not wanting to be the one in charge.

"No, wait, let me guess." He holds me against the wall as he uses his own feet to kick mine further apart.

I let him, of course, gripping the wall behind me with my fingernails so hard, I worry about damaging my rental.

When his hand reaches down to roughly pull the bottom hem of my skirt a bit higher, I can't hold it in any longer. A whimper slips through my lips, followed by a single word.

"Please."

Wes hears it for the beg that it is.

His hand moves up between my legs and inside my drenched panties quicker than I'm prepared for, and I whimper again as he drags his fingers through my wetness.

"Is all this for me?" he asks.

I'm humiliated and angry and terrified and so turned on. All I can do is moan as he presses his fingers inside me.

It's been so long since I've had anything in there that wasn't made of silicone, I almost forgot what it feels like to be out of control. To be in someone else's hands—literally. It hurts a little as he opens me with his fingers, but I want it to hurt. I let my eyes drop closed and imagine the delicious stretch of his cock inside me.

"Jesus fucking Christ, Julia" Wes growls out as he starts to pump his fingers in and out.

I want to be cool. I want to take it like a pro and show him what I'm made of, but as soon as his thumb touches down on my clit, fingers deep inside my pussy, I know it's going to be over soon.

"Harder," I manage to get out between gasping breaths.

"Which hand?" Wes jokes darkly, leaning over to bite down on the meat of my shoulder.

"Both fucking hands, Wes," I gasp.

And he delivers.

He must have all four fingers stretching me open as he thrusts in and out, still massaging my clit with his thumb. And he closes his grip around my neck in a terrifyingly satisfying way.

I actually cannot draw a breath.

I let the feeling of panic overtake me, drive me to madness, as my eyes widen and my mouth falls open in a big, round O.

My core buckles as I come, driving me forward into his hand so hard I nearly see stars. Wes shoves me back against the wall and works me through my orgasm, holding me firmly by the neck as he fucks me with his fingers.

It ends too soon and not soon enough. I grasp his wrist with both hands and pull him off my neck, gasping and choking as oxygen fills my lungs.

He remains there, chest pressed flat to mine, hand buried in my dripping pussy, as I catch my breath.

Just when my lungs start to think they're out of the woods, I feel Wes's rough chin graze across mine, his warm lips trailing just under my still-parted lips.

My whole body seizes with anticipation as I wait to see if he's going to...

"Got any other books, Poppins?" He growls the whisper, still so close I can feel the wind of his breath across my needy, unkissed lips.

I shake myself out of it, taking a step to the side to get some distance.

Wes's hands fall away and suddenly, still flushed from my orgasm, I'm freezing.

What was I thinking allowing this near stranger to see the most vulnerable parts of me?

I straighten my skirt and re-button my blouse, determined to bring us back on level footing the only way I know how. Work. "I could write a book called *How I Got Fired after Failing to Keep an Insane Old Newspaper Critic Happy for One Goddamn Week.*"

But Wes just shakes his head, not taking the bait. Not allowing me to change the subject.

As I watch in horror—and also, full disclosure, sick pleasure—he licks his fingers clean. "You're not going to fool me with this uptight act anymore, Jules. I know the truth."

"You know nothing," I bark, grabbing the two heavy bags from the kitchen counter and marching toward the door. I hold it open expectantly, not about to leave him alone in here for one second.

Wes strolls casually across my house, taking one of the bags from me as he passes into the night.

I have to pause to catch my breath after his shoulder brushes past my still peaked nipple as he exits. His fingers curl to drag across the front of my skirt.

I swallow hard and start to close the door, but make a last minute, split-second decision that I'm sure I'll come to regret.

Stepping inside, I pull one more book off the shelf and hide it deep down in the bag of groceries. Then I shut off the light and lock the door behind me.

Rule #6

KEEP YOUR HEAD ABOVE WATER

WES

THERE ARE MUCH WORSE ways to die than in the aqua blue ocean, on a dazzling Christmas Eve. Not a cloud in the sky. Calm waters and reggae Christmas playing softly from the boat sound system.

Because if Jules was lying about being able to pilot this baby, that's what we're all going to be. Dead.

"All aboard!" she shouts cheerfully as I walk Margo down the dock.

I spent the morning prepping lunch for our ill-advised trip to sea. Boiled eggs and fruit, cheese sandwiches, and homemade shortbread cookies I'd rolled out and baked at the very height of my sexual frustration.

I'd required two separate stints in the shower last night, jerking off to the memory of my hand around her neck. The way her body opened for me.

More than once, I considered trying to figure out which room she was camping out in…

But that was before I found the book.

It could have been an honest mistake. A token leftover from a past picnic she forgot to take out of the tote.

It could also have been a message.

A message I'm both intrigued...and a little terrified...to decipher.

One thing I know for certain—nothing is going to get in the way of me finding out.

And that's why, when I was up at the crack of dawn and discovered a hand-written note from the generator technician taped to the locked front doors, letting us know he needed to have access to the property later this morning to get the systems back up and running...I pocketed the message without sharing it.

When he arrives to try to turn the power back on, we'll be out at sea.

There's something going on between me and Jules, and I'm not about to let ten thousand lightbulbs ruin it.

"Slow down, jackass!" Margo barks at me.

I stop short, only just now realizing I'd been practically dragging the old lady behind me in my hurry to get into the boat.

"My apologies, Ms. Vale. I don't know what's gotten into me this morning."

She pulls her arm out of my grasp and smirks up at me. "You and I both know that's a load of crap."

I open my mouth to protest, but she just hops onto the boat, cackling at her own little joke.

"You sure about this?" I ask as I slide into the passenger seat at the front of the boat.

It's the first thing I've said to Julia since we left her house last night. She pulled a Houdini-worthy disappearing act after ditching me with the groceries just inside the front door of the hotel, and she's been expertly avoiding my gaze—perfect smile plastered in place—since we started loading the boat.

"Sure that our guest deserves a special holiday snorkel trip at Honeymoon Cove? Yes, Wes. I'm sure."

"You know why they call it that, right? Honeymoon Cove?"

"Oh, get a room, you two," Margo barks from the rear of the boat, where she's reclining on a bench, first cocktail of the day in hand.

Jules blushes bright red and turns the key with a bit more force then seems necessary.

We only hit one buoy and graze the side of the other resort snorkel boat as we pull out into the bay. I'd give her hell for it, but she's just so darn cute in her ball cap and aviators, lip clenched tightly between her teeth in concentration.

I've gotta say, after ten minutes with my hand inside her, and ten hours of picturing what she looks like naked and spread out before me, my perception of this woman has changed entirely. It's not that she was never my type, not exactly. I just tend to go for more of the ask no questions, no strings attached situations. It's the only way I can make sure to stay focused on my goals.

But I'll be damned if madame *"settle down and take life seriously"* hasn't wedged her way so far into my lizard brain that I actually made my cot and straightened up my basement hideaway this morning. Just in case.

"What are you looking at?" Julia snipes at me.

I look away quickly as I realize I've been staring for God only knows how long. "Just wondering if that radio could be used to contact the cruise ship the owners are on."

"As if we'd ever be able to locate the right channel."

I shrug. I no longer have any desire to escape our predicament, and I know damn well she's not overly concerned with being rescued...but teasing her is just too fun to give it up. "Be worth a try. We could at least send out a mayday."

"We aren't in trouble," she offers cautiously, clearly feeling out how serious I am.

I decide to give her a break. "We'd be in a heck of a lot of trouble if anyone ever found out we took a guest on this boat."

"They wouldn't be mad. They'd be grateful we showed our VIP guest a good time," she hisses at me, tossing a glance backward toward said guest, who doesn't seem to be listening...but you never can tell with that one.

"Right. And then you'd get that promotion you've been hoping for."

Her head turns sharply toward me, and the boat lurches sharply as well.

"Eye on the destination, Julia."

Her glare burns two holes in the side of my head. "I know how to drive a boat."

"And why is that?"

She pauses, feigning interest in the horizon. But I'm nothing if not patient. And this little vixen is officially my new, much unneeded, distraction.

"I grew up on the coast. Oregon. My grandparents had a house on the beach with a dock. We had a boat kinda like this one actually. Except it was off-white, brown, and yellow. From the seventies." She laughs to herself at the memory.

"Sounds amazing."

Julia nods, meeting my gaze for the first time since she caught me with that book in my hand. For a moment, there's a familiarity between us. A calm understanding I haven't felt before, between the tension of our little work arrangement and…the other tension. "It was."

"Why'd you leave?" Three little words, and I ruin it.

She looks away. "We're almost there," she calls back to Margo.

It takes all three of us to tie the boat to the buoy in Honeymoon Bay. Jules to steer, me to try to catch the buoy and tie us up, and Margo to stand at the back of the boat and tell us we're doing it wrong. It takes all of my strength not to spin around and tell her she can do it herself if she likes, but I persevere.

When it's over, the boat secured, and our grumpy old lady happily strapping on her fins, I feel proud of myself for keeping my cool. Customer service has never been my forte, but it's going to have to be soon enough.

"What's the plan?" I ask Julia, because she clearly has one.

"When I came out on this trip, the guide swam everyone to the beach with the coolers on this big ring and then people snorkeled from there. We just need to swim right down the center of the bay, through the split in the reef. Can you see it?"

I nod. It's easy to see the dark reef contrasted against the white sand through the clear water from our vantage point in the boat. I know from experience that it's going to be much more difficult to see once we're in the water.

I get in first and hold the loaded ring while Margo swings herself over the side of the boat.

"Quite a drop," she calls out. The first hint of weakness I've seen from the old lady.

"It looks higher than it is. Just push off with your hands, and you'll drop down. It's only about two feet."

I'm just awarding myself yet another shiny customer

service badge when Jules finishes securing the boat and starts stripping down to her bikini.

Her breasts are round and full in the black top, spilling over just enough to give me something to bite down on…

Splash!

Margo nearly lands on my head as she finally makes the leap.

She goes straight under as I struggle to keep hold of the floating cooler ring and reach down to drag her back to the surface.

"There you are," I reassure her as I latch one of her hands to the ring. "Wasn't so bad, was it?"

"You were so busy ogling the captain, I nearly drowned."

I crack a sly smile. "Yeah, well, we all have our priorities, don't we?"

It's a completely inappropriate thing to say to a guest, especially since I more or less just admitted to negligence, but Margo smiles back, just like I knew she would.

"Oh, to be young and stupid again."

"I'll make the most of it for both of us."

"Promise?"

I grin as my attention shifts to Julia, who is sitting on the side of the boat, purple fins dangling into the water. She's pulled on a black, long-sleeved, sun shirt, which covers some of the skin I've been fantasizing about running my teeth over, but the thing is skintight, the shiny material stretched over the curves and dips of her torso and breasts, and somehow just makes me want her more.

"Promise," I tell Margo.

The old lady busies herself getting her towel and umbrella set up while Jules and I drag the coolers up the beach to a shady spot under a palm tree.

"Whew," I sigh, shaking my head and pausing to catch my breath in the glorious shade.

"Wore yourself out already? It's only nine a.m." Julia narrows her eyes at me, hands on her hips.

"I was up late last night."

She won't look at me now, busying herself opening and closing both coolers as if checking to make sure everything's there.

I smile as I deliver my next line. "Reading."

Her eyes dart up to meet mine, but only for the briefest moment. I catch surprise and fear and a little curiosity. Then she's back to business.

"Let's get the water bottles filled and leave the rest of this stuff for after we've been in the water for a while." None of it needs to be said, but I'm starting to understand the pattern of this woman's emotions. She gets scared and takes charge of something—anything—in order to feel in control.

But I got a little sneak peek of her real desire last night.

I know damn well she's dying to lose some of that tightly wound control.

"I'm going in," Margo calls, already stepping into the gently lapping waves, apparently not concerned with waiting for us.

"Stay inside the reef," Jules calls, hurrying down the beach toward her, ice-cold water bottle in hand.

"I've been snorkeling since before you were born, girlie," Margo huffs.

I flop down on my towel and watch Jules watching Margo swim off. I can almost feel the tension she holds in that beautiful, curvy body. From the way her fingers grip into her hips to her locked-knees stance, she's practically radiating nerves.

"She'll be fine, Jules," I call out.

Julia spins on me. I can't see her eyes behind those mirrored sunglasses, but her pursed lips let me know I'm about to get read the riot act.

Instead, she softens before my eyes, dropping her arms to her sides and walking up the beach to collapse on her own striped towel. "I should go in with her," she comments, making no move to get up.

"We'll go in a few," I tell her, leaning back to rest on my elbows. "She didn't seem all that interested in having company."

"She just looks so lonely."

I shake my head. "Again, Jules, alone and lonely are two different things. Lonely is something we project onto other people. Be honest, when was the last time you were swimming alone or sunbathing on a private beach, or out on a walk, or even in your house reading a book, and thought to yourself, I feel lonely?"

She doesn't answer, but I can see my words land. I watch her take a long, slow inhale, filling her lungs before sighing it out. "You're right. I don't feel lonely when I'm alone."

She swallows hard, and I sense there's more, so I wait.

"I feel lonely, though. A lot. When I'm at work. When I'm out with friends. When I'm back in The States with my family."

Her statement contains so much pain and raw honesty, I'm stunned silent.

Which is just as well, I suppose, because she's not done breaking my heart.

"I guess you're right that I wouldn't feel lonely out snorkeling by myself. I'd feel lonely on the boat ride back, when everyone was telling their families about the fish they saw, and I'd just be scrolling through my underwater camera shots, knowing damn well I don't have anyone to show them to."

"Jules." It's more of an exhalation. I breathe her name, wanting her to know that I hear her pain. That I bear witness to her honesty.

But she buttons right back up. "It's fine. I don't need your pity."

She starts to push herself up off the beach, and I take hold of her wrist and pull her back down.

It's not something I'd ever considered doing to a woman before in my life.

It's the kind of act I might've punched a guy for.

But something's shifted between us.

Sure, it started last night, when I pinned her to the wall, and she bloomed like a flower.

But it really came into focus right now, when she shared something I have a feeling she's never shared before.

It only feels right to reciprocate. "I feel lonely when I think about the future."

Jules lays her head on her bent knees, facing me. I still can't see her eyes through her mirrored glasses, but I'm almost grateful for that.

"I keep everything I do a secret. It just feels like the only way not to have my dreams stolen from me. So, I work and I hang out, and all the while I keep all my big plans to myself. I work hard toward them when no one is around, and I know people will be surprised and confused when I just disappear. It really makes me understand that none of my friends are really my friends. They just don't know it yet."

Julia pulls off her sunglasses and meets my gaze.

The silence stretches long and heated between us.

Finally, she blinks and shakes her head gently. "Thank you for sharing that with me."

I shrug. "I figured I owed you a deep dark secret. After last night."

She blows out her breath and turns back to the water. I feel her closing down again, so I catch her arm once more before she can escape.

"You need a safe word, Poppins."

The statement hangs in the air for a long moment, neither of us quite able to believe I just said it.

Julia finally recovers and apparently decides to pretend she has no idea what I'm talking about. "Excuse me?"

I'm not buying it. "A safe word. Choose one. Now."

Julia slides her shades back on and pushes to her feet, brushing the sand off her butt.

I brace myself for the white-hot sear of her rejection as she starts to walk away.

"Mistletoe," she says, turning back to me from a few feet down the beach.

"Mistletoe?" I fail to hide the laughter from my voice.

"Yes, mistletoe. It's fucking Christmas, Wes."

And so it is.

We all manage to avoid getting sunburned and spend the boat ride home cataloging our favorite fish from the day.

Margo claims to have seen a tiny reef octopus. She swears she tried to call us over, but we were too busy searching for "trouser eels."

Julia tells us about a queen angelfish she saw darting through the gap between the reef sections, heading out to deeper waters.

I know exactly what my favorite sighting was on this snorkel trip. It was an elusive, carefree Julia.

But I can't say that now, can I?

I show them a picture I snapped of a flamingo tongue snail and accept their oohs and ahhs as a consolation prize.

Because I know my real gift is waiting somewhere in this big, empty resort.

And tonight, I'm going to unwrap it.

Rule #7

DON'T SKIP THE SLOW DANCE

JULIA

WES PULLS OUT ALL the stops for a beautiful Christmas Eve dinner spread, even though the damn technicians still haven't shown up to turn the power back on.

Honestly, though, the quiet, sunlit resort is starting to grow on me. Usually, the windows and doors are closed tight to keep the A/C running properly. Without the climate control, every room is filled with billowing curtains and ocean breeze.

I decorate the dining area with extra sparkle. A red tablecloth and candles on every surface. Even our grumpy guest can't help but smile when she enters the room after her nap, dressed in soft black pants and what could only be described as an "ugly" Christmas blouse.

I'm fully prepared for her to invite us to dine with her, but she doesn't, reading her book as she makes her way through all seven of the gourmet courses Wes managed to scrape together from our combined groceries. He and I eat each course as well, sitting together on stools behind the bar.

"Favorite Christmas song?" I ask as we sip mulled wine and wait for Margo to finish her third course.

Wes cringes. "None of them. You?"

I shrug bashfully. "Carol of the Bells."

His face twists in confusion. "I don't know that one. Sing it for me."

I scoff out a laugh. As if. "It's the spooky choir one. They used it in *Home Alone*. You must remember that movie."

"Oh, the witchy orchestra one? Merry merry merry merry Christmas!" He does his best impression of the over-the-top choir song, and it's actually pretty spot on.

I laugh so hard, warm wine nearly comes out of my nose. "Yes! That's it."

He nods side to side. "I guess that one's pretty cool."

Silence falls, and I nearly panic, but Wes is one step ahead of me.

"Favorite Christmas movie?" he asks.

"Easy. *White Christmas*." I hold up my hand before he can name his. "I swear to god, Wes, if you say *A Christmas Story*, I'm kicking you to the curb."

A sly smile spreads over his deliciously handsome face. "Is that all it would have taken to get out of this whole thing?" He clucks his tongue. "Wish I'd known that yesterday."

I get his joke, but the jovial mood is ruined. He can feel it too, and, to his credit, he tries to save it. "It's a classic. What's not to like?"

I glance up and catch Margo's impatient gaze. Grateful for an excuse to leave, I hop to my feet and head out to fill her wine.

We've put together the best Christmas Eve activity we could think of for a single old woman who prefers to be left alone, and it's the only thing we could come up with without power.

I set up a comfy deck sofa in the gazebo at the end of the dock, and Wes ran an extension cord from the single gas-powered generator all the way out there so we could play a record he produced from goodness knows where—the *Christmas Sing with Bing* recording from 1955.

I'm just lighting the last of the hurricane candles as Wes walks Margo down the dock, bottle of sherry and three glasses in hand.

"This is beautiful," she whispers as he guides her to the sofa.

Wes and I settle onto the wooden bench along the edge of the gazebo and lean back against the railing, sipping sherry as we watch the stars twinkle to life.

When Bing Crosby's deep, rich baritone sings the opening line of "White Christmas," I can hear Margo sobbing softly.

"How did you know?" I whisper to Wes.

I feel him shrug in the darkness. "It just seemed right."

"This was my grandparents' favorite song. They had a Christmas Eve wedding actually. A small one before he left for the war. They danced to this song then, and it was always a tradition for them to dance to it on Christmas Eve." I feel my own tears start to rise as I remember joining in as a kid and then watching from the sofa as I grew older, wondering if I'd ever find a love like that.

No one else seemed to have it, and it was impossible for my young mind to determine what exactly they were doing differently. The only thing I knew was that the two of them were the hardest workers I'd ever met. They retired from blue-collar jobs with nice retirement accounts. Even into their eighties, their home and vehicles were in pristine condition. Their gardens were bursting with colorful flowers and sun-ripened straw-berries.

I decided from a young age that hard work must be the ticket to true love, and I set out to replicate their success.

Now, as an exhausted, disillusioned adult, I wonder if there was an error in my understanding of this life lesson.

I keep working harder and harder and all I seem to get is more responsibility—and therefore more work.

Wes is still watching me, so I bring my glass up to give his the tiniest little clink. A thank you for helping me make this night so special.

He sips the delicious, sweet wine along with me before rising to his feet and pulling me up after him.

The gazebo spins just a bit as he takes my hand and places his other on my hip, guiding me into the gentle beat of the song.

I'm dreaming of a White Christmas. Just like the ones I used to know...

We pad barefoot across the wooden deck, swaying and grinning and laughing softly as he spins me and catches me tightly in his arms again and again.

When the song ends and Bing and friends begin their old-timey holiday banter and storytelling once more, I stand frozen, unable to let go.

"I'm staying in room—" I start.

"Don't," he interrupts me with an abrupt whisper.

My heart literally stops beating for a moment.

Did I read this whole thing wrong?

I'm about to melt into a puddle of shame when he speaks again.

"I'll find you. That's how the story goes."

The fear that was roiling in my belly only seconds before morphs into a fire that threatens to burn me alive.

That is, indeed, how the story goes.

And it sounds like I'm going to get my fairytale.

Rule #8

KEEP IT IN CHARACTER

JULIA

I CAN ALMOST RECITE the scene from memory, that's how many times I've read the novel.

The book is a tantalizing slow burn, filled with bickering banter and tension, that leads up to the night of their arranged marriage. After the ceremony, the heroine goes to the bathroom—and sneaks down the back hallway to lock herself in one of the rooms of the hotel. She knows the property is too well guarded to escape, so she resigns to hiding in one of the unused rooms until her evil new husband decides she must have somehow escaped and goes elsewhere to search for her.

In the book, there's a storm on the evening of the wedding, creating a dramatic thunder and lightning backdrop to the forced vows. And, just as the corrupt priest is announcing them as husband and wife, the power goes out.

We, of course, haven't had power for days, and when the air turns crisp and the rain starts as we're finishing clearing the gazebo, I start to get really excited.

"Be sure to lock the dead bolt on your patio doors, Margo. There's a storm coming," I remind our guest as she makes her way down the hallway to her room, flashlight in hand.

All things considered, the woman has turned out to be a pretty good sport.

Which is handy, considering tonight, I plan to be hunted for sport.

I'm not sure how Wes will figure out which room I'm in. For all I know, he's always known. I make sure to sneak up to my oceanfront, two-bedroom suite on the second floor extra quietly, just in case.

Taking a quick shower to shave my legs, I slip into the only thing I have that's even remotely appropriate for my role as the semi-virginal new bride of a Mafia boss. I say semi because, of course, he already took her throat in a dramatic bridal suite scene before the ceremony. Everyone told him it was bad luck to see the bride before the wedding. He responded that you make your own luck and proceeded to bolt the doors and order her to her knees.

With a grin and a shiver, I wonder if I'll ever get to recreate that particular scene.

Footsteps in the hall come before I'm ready.

I flip off the flashlight and cap my shiny pink lip gloss in the dark, tiptoeing out of the bathroom and into the ocean-side bedroom. It's spacious, with a tall, wicker wardrobe where I plan to hide. The woman in the book made a similar choice, hiding behind the ironing board in a closet. It always struck me as not the smartest place. I mean, it leaves you no way to run if you get caught. But she did end up getting some running in. And I plan to as well.

Excitement and nerves swell to fill my chest as I play through the scene in my mind.

I have no reason to be scared. It's only a game.

But when I hear the door to my hotel room slam open, I have to stifle a gasp.

"I know you're in here, wife."

Any tingling sensations I'd been calling fear morph straight into burning desire as Wes calls out the iconic, famously quoted line from the book.

I hold my breath.

"I can smell you."

Keeping my breathing as low and even as I can, I listen to him storm the suite, opening and slamming every possible door I could be hiding behind, flipping furniture, shaking out drapes.

He's not wearing fancy dress shoes like the man in the book, but I still hear the scuff of his sneakers as he crosses the bedroom toward where I hide, crouched behind my hanging work uniforms in the wardrobe.

He throws open the doors of the closet next to me, the motion rattling my hiding place and sending chills through my body.

"You could make this whole thing a lot easier if you'd just come out," he calls in a low voice, trying to sound calm but clearly masking anger.

"What kind of bride hides on her wedding night?"

The closet slams closed, and I jump a little, despite myself.

I hear him thrashing through the bedclothes, making sure I'm not under the bed, and pulling back the long drapes.

A little metallic rattle lets me know he unlatched the big windows overlooking the ocean. The sound of rain and crashing waves gets louder. A bolt of lightning lights up the crack at the bottom of the wardrobe doors and thunder booms.

I place my hand on my chest to still my racing heart.

I'm so focused on trying to hear his footsteps over the raging storm that it takes me completely by surprise when the doors fly open.

My cry of terror is real.

Wes grabs my wrist and drags me out of the cabinet so quickly, I don't get my feet under myself in time and fall to my knees before scrambling back up to standing.

"You trying to make a fool out of me?" he growls.

I shake my head, trying as hard as I can to twist my wrist from his grasp, but he holds tight. As I flail, he reaches out and captures my other arm, walking backward and dragging me toward the bed.

"I told everyone at the party you were just so eager to get upstairs to our honeymoon suite. They all think you're quite the little slut, so they had no trouble believing me."

"Let me go!" I cry, uttering my first words and shocking myself with how truly distressed I sound.

Wes's mouth twists into a grim smile in the dim light of the flashlight he tossed onto the bed. "You belong to me now, wife. You can run. You can hide. But wherever you go, I'll find you."

"I hate you!" I scream.

"That's fine. Plenty of people do."

He uses his grasp on my arms to force me down onto the bed…and then makes a fatal error. As he releases one of my arms to try to get my legs to swing up to a lying position, I use all my pent-up energy to twist—and manage to get my other hand free.

I'm on my feet in an instant, stumbling once as I launch myself toward the open door.

The doorframe clips my shoulder as I pass through, sending a jolt of pain through my body, but I'm running on pure adrenaline now, and it doesn't slow me in the slightest.

Wes catches me before I even cross the living room, taking me down onto the sofa with his entire body, straddling my hips to pin me in a seated position as he recaptures my arms. He shifts both of my wrists to one of his big, strong hands, while he pulls his silk tie loose.

Where this man got a tie for tonight, I don't know, but I'm not sad about it.

One of my wrists breaks free, and I get a swing in, my forearm connecting hard with his left temple. Snarling, he forces my arms back together and lifts slightly to roll me facedown beneath him. He binds my hands behind my back with the silk tie as I continue to struggle.

When he rolls me back over to face him, his expression is pure evil.

"I could have had any woman in the world, do you know that?"

"You should have picked a nicer one, I guess." I spit the words at him, my loose, messy hair in my eyes and mouth.

Wes reaches up to smooth it behind my ears on each side. "I didn't want a nice one, lover."

"I'm not your lover."

"Oh, but you will be. It's no fun at all to take a woman who's just offering it to you. No, the real sweetness comes when you have to break her."

"You'll never break me."

His smile widens, and he clicks his tongue as he reaches down and takes the hemline of my silky camisole in both fists, tearing it just enough to expose my breasts. "I'm not sure if you've noticed, *wife*." Wes hisses the last word at me, drawing the f out until I feel his soft breath on my peaked nipples. "But I always get what I want."

With a loud rip, he tears the rest of my top in half, taking my breasts in both hands. "I've been waiting a long time to get you naked."

I struggle harder, but it's no use. Between the weight of his body straddling my hips and my arms tied tightly behind my back, I have no chance of breaking free.

Wes reaches up to gather my long hair in his hands, winding the tangled mess around one of his hands and pulling hard, forcing me to look up at him. "Don't tell me you've already forgotten my little visit to your room earlier. You told me you'd never open that pretty little mouth for me, but in the end, you did."

I can barely breathe now, suspense and anticipation warring in my chest cavity, both trying to kill me from lack of oxygen.

"I could have taken care of you then, given you something nice to think about during our vows, but I wanted to make you wait. I knew you'd want me just as much afterward."

"I don't want you," I hiss through my clenched jaw as he pulls my hair tighter with one hand...

And reaches between my legs with the other.

"We'll just see about that, won't we?"

I try to struggle free once more, but the pain from his grip on my hair keeps me still, my eyes watering.

"Don't cry, lover. I'll make sure you like it."

The little black silk shorts I have on give zero resistance as he works his fingers up one of the short leg holes.

I don't own a single pair of underwear I deemed worthy of this night, so I went with none. It's a bit off script, but Wes doesn't miss a beat.

He growls as his fingers slide right into my slick wetness. "She's waiting in a dark hotel suite, wearing a tiny, silky negligee and no panties..."

I gasp as his fingers push roughly inside me.

"And claims she doesn't want me."

He tsk tsks with his tongue as he pulls out and brings

his glisteningly wet fingers up to the soft, golden light of the battery-powered lantern on the coffee table. "What's all this?"

"I hate you," I tell him again, but it has less bite this time.

"Well, if this is what hate does to your pretty little pussy, I think I'll keep you hating me for as long as possible."

I thrash again in another burst of energy, pain in my scalp be damned.

"I've never been known as a merciful man, but those who are able to get some perspective will tell you I am fair."

"Is that what you call threatening to kill my family if I didn't marry you? Fair?"

He nods. "I could have just killed them, you know. I didn't need to offer anything to you."

My watering eyes blink furiously as actual tears start to form and roll down my cheeks.

Wes cocks his head, expression hardening as his eyes narrow. "But since it's our wedding night, I'm going to give you what you want. Doesn't that seem fair?"

"You have no idea what I want."

"It seems to me, wife, that right now, you want to run."

Anticipation swells in my chest as he speaks the heavily highlighted words.

"You...you'd let me go?"

"If you ask me nicely."

"P-please," I sob.

"Please what, wife?"

"Please let me go."

He releases my hair first, and I nearly sigh with relief. He then pushes up and off my lap, backing up until he stands a few feet away, still watching me like a hawk, arms crossed over his chest.

In the dim light, he looks devastatingly handsome in a white tux shirt, unbuttoned enough to show the tops of the black tattoos that cover his chest. His hair is tousled from the struggle, and his blue eyes glitter darkly, like the night sky after a storm passes.

Tentatively, I struggle to my own feet. "Will you untie my hands?"

He just shakes his head slowly.

I take a step backward, nearly tripping over the couch as I misjudge its length. I continue to back away from him until my bound hands find the door. It takes a bit of maneuvering to lift the metal handle, but I manage, and swing the door open behind me.

I take one tentative step backward into the hallway.

Wes hasn't moved.

I take another, into the shadows of the dark hall, leaving the lantern light behind.

We both stand still for a moment that seems to stretch on forever.

Finally, with a deep breath, I run.

I should have chosen to run toward the elevator bank, where there's a stairwell, but I know it would have been impossible to get the door open before he caught me.

My feet pound down the tile of the long, second-story hallway toward the massive window at the end.

I count my steps.

One, two, three, fo—

Wes's heavy footfalls enter the hallway and gain on me much faster than I was expecting.

I scream as I try to pick up speed, but it's no use.

He grabs me around the middle as I'm passing the last door in the hall, pressing my face against the glass pane of the storm windows.

"You said you'd let me go," I sob, cheek pressed flat against the cool glass.

"And I did, wife. I'm a man of my word."

"But..."

"But?" he taunts me, using the hand not pinned around the back of my neck to shove my shorts down around my thighs. "But I also told you that if you ran..."

His fingers are inside me once more, gripping my body and pulling my hips to meet his as he slides his other hand to the front of my neck and pulls me flat against his chest.

I can barely breathe with his hand wrapped around my neck. I squeeze my eyes closed and sob, adrenaline still coursing through my veins.

"...I'd catch you."

He pulls his hand out of my pussy and reaches up to unlatch the two big windows, his wet fingers leaving a humiliating smear over the glass as he pushes them wide open.

The raging wind drives a blast of cold rain into my face as the sky lights up with jagged purple lightning and thunder booms.

"I was planning to let you off easy for your first time. Some roses, candles, and soft caresses as I took you."

He grips my hair once more, forcing me to bend forward until my whole upper half is outside the second-story window. I want to scream, but his other hand grips my neck, holding me still as he bends over to whisper in my ear.

"But this is a much more fitting arrangement. It's almost like a metaphor for the rest of your life, lover. When given a choice, you chose to sacrifice yourself. I hope you're happy with the consequences of your actions."

I shake my head, and Wes loosens his hand enough for

me to speak. "What do you mean I had a choice? Marry you or my family dies is hardly a fair choice."

"It would have meant freedom either way. Turn me down, and you would have stepped into power at the head of your family. Free from their control and hatred. Free to use your fortune as you wished. But you chose me."

"B-but why did you choose me?" I gasp out, my teeth starting to chatter from the rain and wind still pelting my face.

"I chose you because you're the only woman I've ever met in this world who had any fight left in her."

"And you wanted to snuff it out."

"No, wife. Quite the opposite. I knew you were destined for greatness. For power. Who wouldn't want you standing by their side?"

I close my eyes as the shift happens, as we play out the dramatic scene of a powerful man and his prisoner becoming equals.

My heart is racing because I know exactly what comes next.

I have my word.

Mistletoe...

I could stop this at any moment.

Instead, I deliver the line that seals my fate. "I'll never stand beside you."

Wes, as wrapped up in all of this as I am, pulls my body back and holds me tightly against his chest, whispering in my ear. "You'll stand beside me until you understand your own power. Then, wife, you'll rule beside me."

He shifts my legs wider with his own legs, and I feel his hand enter me once more. He slides in so easily, if I had a drop of shame left, it would be burning my cheeks right now.

But I don't feel ashamed.

I feel powerful and alive.

The slide of his zipper is the ultimate punctuation to the storm raging outside.

My breath catches as I feel him line himself up at my entrance, swirling his tip to open me.

"I quite like being the first man to take you, wife." Wes pushes upward, using his height to slide his tip inside me an inch or so. "And I'll spend the rest of my life making sure I'm the last, as well."

Delivering the steamy, claiming line nearly word-for-word, Wes slides himself home.

It's all I can do not to moan aloud as he stretches me open. I only felt his hardness pressed against me through his clothes last night, but I knew he'd be this big. It's almost too big, but I take it. I savor the warm sting of my body making room for his invasion.

Arm wrapped tightly around my center, holding me close to him, Wes pulls out and thrusts upward, again and again until I'm lost in the rhythm of it.

It's so inappropriate. So unlike me. So, so dangerous to be fucking in the hallway of the resort, a guest sleeping just downstairs. But I can't bring myself to stop him. All I want is more.

My hands are still bound, so I rely entirely on Wes to keep me upright as he pounds into me. The strength of his arms around me is the safest I've ever felt. I close my eyes and lose myself entirely in the moment.

"You feel incredible," he groans out as he thrusts into me once more.

I want to agree, to tell him this is the most alive I've ever felt, but I can't manage the words.

One of his hands drops down between my legs and his strong fingers press into my clit as his thrusts rock my body against his grip.

It's the second time in two days he's going to make me come standing up, pressed against a wall, and I open my mouth to make a joke about it, but the swell of laughter I feel rising from my belly morphs into an orgasm, and I can't speak. My core contracts as I buck against his hand, crying out much louder than I expect. I groan and gasp and do not know who this woman I've apparently become is.

"That's it, wife. Show me who owns this pretty little pussy."

The line is completely improvised, but I'm so into it, I can't even be mad. I just keep coming, my gasps catching in my throat as I ride wave after wave of forbidden pleasure, right out in the open where anyone could see.

"That's my girl," Wes murmurs, and it's Wes again. The Wes I've been arguing with and working with and secretly drooling over.

"Wes," I whisper.

"Don't worry, I got you," he whispers back. I can hear the strain in his voice. I know he's close.

He holds me closer than ever, thrusting hard as he approaches his own cliff.

"Once I claim you," he growls out, breathless but still committed to our little game. "I'll never let you go."

I could stop him.

I should stop him.

But right now, it's painfully obvious how much I really do want to be claimed.

And not just by anyone.

By this man.

I inhale and arch my back, tilting to increase his friction, and feel myself expand as his warmth explodes inside me. He pumps through it, moaning my name—my actual name —as he fills me. Claims me as his own.

I do feel like the queen now.

And I never want this feeling to end.

Wes loosens his grip around my chest, and I sag forward, head turning so my cheek presses against the glass of the open window as he grips my hips with both hands and finishes with long, powerful thrusts in and out of me. I feel every centimeter of his length, his hard tip grazing through the sensitive folds of my body.

All good things must come to an end.

He pulls out, and I feel his wet, still-hard cock rest on my lower back as he reaches down to pull my body back against his chest.

Using his damp fingers, he brushes my hair back so he can press his lips to my ear, my cheek. I can smell myself, both of us, on his hand and suddenly, I'm ready to go again.

But nothing could prepare me for what he says next.

"Marry me."

I smile and huff a small laugh as he stumbles in the script. "They're already married. Remember?"

Wes shakes his head, and I feel it against my own, his forehead still pressing into my hair. "I'm serious, Julia. Marry me."

I tense and clamp my mouth closed to keep from falling for it and saying yes.

He must be joking.

"You don't even know me," I whisper.

"I know you're ferociously strong and dedicated," Wes starts, reaching down to gently untie my arms. I wrap them around my center, and he hugs me even tighter. "I know you're lonely around other people, just like me. But you keep showing up."

My eyes drop closed as tears start to well. They're happy tears. Emotional tears. Overwhelmed tears. Tears from finally being seen.

Wes reaches down and scoops me into his arms, our

eyes meeting for the first time since we started this game. "I know calling you wife felt like the truest statement I've ever made."

I hold his gaze, searching for the joke.

I find only genuine emotion. The same strength and commitment I've seen in his eyes these last few days. As he helped me pull off this crazy stunt, even when he could have run. As he showed up to support me every step of the way.

"Can I think about it?" I whisper.

His face breaks into a wide smile, and my heart lurches. "You better think about it. I'm not going to let you think about anyone else for a long time."

He carries me back to the hotel suite where I've set up camp and walks us straight into the giant, walk-in steam shower. Setting me down on the marble tile bench, he proceeds to remove my soaked, torn clothing, delicately draping them over the bar on the wall.

Wes turns the water on hot and kneels on the shower floor between my knees. I watch as he lathers a washcloth with the fancy plumeria body wash from the bottle on the shelf and begins to rub it gently over my thighs, up my torso, across my shoulders, down my arms.

I melt over him, resting my forehead on his head as he touches every part of my body. When he presses my legs apart and lands his tongue on my sensitive clit, I come apart, orgasming as I rock my hips gently back and forth, riding his face and his fingers.

We stay locked in the moment, leaning into each other, the water washing my hair down and over us like a shield against the outside world.

Slowly, slowly, then quickly, the water temperature changes.

Wes pushes to his feet and shuts it off. "I guess we ran through the rest of the hot water in the tank."

I stay seated, tilting my head back as far as it will go to look up at him as he stands over me. Willing this moment not to end. For reality not to take over.

"Don't go," I whisper.

Wes shakes his head, pulling me to my feet and holding my wet, naked body against his. "I'm not going anywhere, wife."

I wake sometime later, chilled, my hair still wet. Soft daylight filters through the sheer curtains as I sit up to drag the heavy quilt from the foot of the bed over us.

When I reach down to brush a lock of Wes's hair off his forehead, he opens his eyes. "Good morning."

"Merry Christmas," I whisper back.

His smile is the only gift I'll ever need. "That's right. I forgot."

I smile back and laugh softly. "How could you forget Christmas?"

He shrugs, reaching up to trace a fingertip over my collarbone and down my arm, leaving a trail of goose bumps in his wake. "I was busy thinking about other things."

I blush softly. "Like claiming me as your wife?" I mean it as a joke but instantly regret uttering the words. My chest seizes with panic as I prepare for him to tell me it was all a game.

But he doesn't.

"That's right."

He sounds so serious, but he must be joking. I decide to change the subject. "How did you memorize that scene so quickly? I mean, it wasn't word for word, but you definitely knew how it was supposed to go, and I only gave you the book yesterday."

"I'd read it before."

I prop myself up on one elbow and gape at him incredulously. "Really?"

I had no idea men would be interested in romance novels.

"It was in the lost and found. I read through all the stuff in the guest library and needed something to do for my long nights in the basement."

"So you'd imagined acting it out before?" That would make a lot of sense. It did seem like he'd practiced.

My heart skips a beat at the idea of him down in the basement, racing through my favorite spicy scenes, hand gripping his own cock, while I was just a few hundred feet away, touching myself to the same words.

"I was a theater geek in high school. Actually got a scholarship and did a year at university in the performing arts department."

"But you dropped out?"

He nods, sad smile forming on his lips. "The scholarship paid my tuition, but I had to work full time to pay for everything else. After a year, I decided I was better off just working."

"But you could have performed in local theater or something. I mean, you clearly have talent."

His smile spreads into a grin. "Glad you enjoyed yourself."

I find myself blushing again and shake my head, punching him softly in the arm. "You know what I mean."

"I thought about it. Auditioned for a few parts. But honestly, I found my new calling in the restaurant industry. There's a certain aspect of performance to that. When I have my own place, it's going to be an open kitchen where people order at the counter, and I get to talk to them. I'll perform all day long."

"I didn't know you wanted to open your own place."

Wes is quiet for a long moment, a far-off look in his eye. When he comes back to the present and rolls to gaze up into my eyes, there's a whole new sparkle there. "We have a lot of getting to know each other to do."

The same uncomfortable ball of tension builds in my chest once more at his insinuation that he wants more than just fun and games during this resort closure. I have to look away before I betray any of the longing probably written right across my face.

I still don't know how I feel about this, let alone what to tell Wes. There's no denying the full body, enthusiastic, soul-level YES! that I received from my intuition when he asked.

But...what if my gut is leading me to heartbreak?

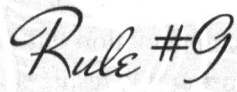

Rule #9

EVERY TREASURE TELLS A STORY

JULIA

WES WAITS BEHIND THE BAR, sipping coffee, as I carry the perfectly plated and garnished banana mango pancakes with toasted coconut out to where Margo lounges on the front deck, underneath the decorated Christmas palm we dragged out there to make it feel festive.

The morning itself is glorious, not too hot, the ocean lapping gently at the beach as gulls fly overhead.

"Merry Christmas, Margo," I beam at her as I set the plate down.

I'm very proud that Wes and I were able to pull off my grandmother's recipe, island-style, and I know this is one thing our grumpy guest won't be able to complain about.

She stares at the plate for a long moment, and I start to panic, wondering if I was mistaken about the complaining.

But when she looks back up at me, her expression has a curious softness. "Are you two joining me?"

My eyes widen in surprise as her tone betrays a hint of

what could be longing. "Oh, we were planning to eat at the bar, but—"

"Well," she quickly averts her gaze, lifting her coffee. "You would be welcome."

"Okay, I'll let Wes know."

"Why on earth would she want us to eat with her?" Wes asks when I tell him.

I shove his plate into one of his hands, his cup of coffee in the other. "Doesn't matter why, Wes. It's Christmas, and this is what she wants."

"What about what I want?" Wes grumbles as he follows me out to the deck.

We settle into a comfy, padded deck sofa and set our plates on the glass table.

"Beautiful morning," Margo says by way of greeting.

"It sure is."

"Heck of a storm last night," she goes on.

"Indeed," I answer, nervous that we're going to spend this meal awkwardly commenting on the weather. But, as I should have expected, Margo has a plan for her words.

"I was up late watching it through the deck doors. Just magnificent. You might want to check on the second floor, though. I think some windows might have blown open. There was quite a racket up there."

Wes nearly chokes trying to swallow a sip of coffee as Margo turns her glittering—knowing—eyes on the two of us.

"I'll head up there after we eat. Make sure nothing... got in."

Margo huffs out a small laugh, taking up her linen napkin roll and placing her silverware neatly beside her plate before folding the napkin in her lap. "Last Christmas, I was at my apartment in Paris. I ordered a lovely spread of croissants and cheese and fruit. I paid the delivery boy to stay and eat with me. I guess it's become a bit of a habit."

I have no idea how to respond to that, and when I glance over at Wes, he looks like he'd rather be anywhere on earth but right here.

I have no choice but to offer up my own pain to soften hers. "Last Christmas, I was at my sister's house. I flew back to The States, even though I'd just started this job and really couldn't afford it. It just felt like what I had to do. It was my first time home for the holidays in a few years. I don't know what I was expecting, but it didn't feel like Christmas. It was just another day of listening to kids fight and cooking for people who didn't really care what we were eating. It made me wonder, though. Was Christmas always just another day? Where did I get the idea that it was so magical in the first place? Must have been childhood delusion."

For a long moment, the only sound is the clinking of silverware against china. I start to panic that I ruined the mood with my depressing account.

"Last Christmas," Wes starts, "I was at the sports bar in town. I don't have much family left, and the ones I do have aren't exactly the hosting sort. There's a group of guys on the island who don't have anywhere to go, and they always get together on the patio outside the bar and spend the morning. Mr. Harlan from Saubry Sweets does a whole spread, and Sal makes spiked eggnog and Irish coffees."

He pauses, far-off look in his eyes.

"It was really interesting to listen to them talk about what the day means. Most had family at one point. Mr. Harlan has an adult son back in The States who he doesn't talk to. Or who doesn't talk to him, I guess. Everyone used to have someone. But the interesting thing is, it didn't sound like they all wished they had it back. They were telling stories of a time in their lives when things were different, but not necessarily better."

"When my brother invited me to come on this retreat with his whole company, I said hell no," Margo says.

We both turn to her in surprise.

She just shrugs. "Stuck in a fancy island resort with a bunch of investment bankers and their screaming kids? Holiday decorations and a full staff all pretending to be happy we were there? Doesn't sound like my idea of a good time."

"What changed your mind?" I ask.

"The snowstorm," Margo admits, a bit sheepishly.

Wes sets down his fork. "Wait, you knew?"

"That the planes were grounded and none of them would make it? Sure, I knew. I may be old, but I still have the internet. Or I did, until I came here."

"We thought you were lonely for Christmas."

"Do I look lonely, girl?"

"I told her you weren't lonely," Wes cuts in.

I shoot him a side glare.

"Lonely is a state of mind," Margo goes on. "One I don't have much use for. Nah, I've been around the world, stayed at all the most exclusive, exotic destination resorts. They've all changed so much. Used to be, people went there to escape. To enjoy themselves. Now, everyone is just there for a photoshoot. It's like they're not really there at all. Might as well be back at home, with a photo backdrop of the ocean, the way they pack all their devices and spend the whole time staring into screens. Used to be, you could go down to breakfast and have a conversation with someone from the other side of the world. Nowadays, everyone's vlogging their meals for their followers. I'm sick of it. I keep saying I'll retire, but I don't know what else to do with myself."

Margo stares out at the ocean, as if the answer to her

problems might come sailing in. After a moment, she shakes her head and sighs. "I left Mexico dead set on never taking another job as long as I lived. That yoga retreat was a total sham. Pure 'content marketing.'" She does the air quotes, a look of disdain on her features. "For yoga teachers trying to build out their own brands. They had these sharing circles, where you were supposed to share the deep personal work you were doing in the meditations and classes, but they held a cell phone camera right up to your face as you talked. I asked them what it was for, and they assured me I could have a copy for my own channel." She spits the word out and shakes her head. "And that I'd signed a photo and video release, so anything I said would be used in their own marketing. I don't want to be marketing. It's bad enough I have to be marketed to all day every day."

Wes and I share a glance as silence falls.

"But then I came here," she adds softly.

My chest tightens as I mentally scan back through the days Margo has been with us, trying to decide if she's going to deem her stay worthy or just another blunder to tear apart online.

"I've known the owners of this resort for years."

I set down my fork as my breakfast turns to lead in my belly at her sudden admission.

Why didn't she tell us she knew the owners?

Would I have acted differently?

I might have tried harder to get a hold of them, to ask them what to do instead of taking on this crazy task and foolishly trying to prove my worth to this place.

"When I got to the water-taxi dock and there was no driver with my name on a sign waiting to pick me up, I figured out my own way. Asked a few locals, hitched a ride. Just like the old days. When I walked up to this place, and it was dark and still, I thought maybe it was siesta. When it became clear that not only were Sam and Dom not here, and they're always here, but there were no other guests, and no power? Only you, Julia, flustered and clearly lying through your teeth? I thought to myself, now this is something I've gotta see. And you two did not disappoint."

My chest releases slightly as I realize I'm probably not going to lose my job over this.

Wes, however, laughs. "What was your favorite part? The illegal snorkel trip or the gas generator-powered coffee maker?"

Margo smiles over at him, warm twinkle in her eye. "My favorite part was watching you two try to pretend you're not crazy for each other."

I feel myself flush as memories of the night before flood my brain. "I'm sorry if we—"

But Margo's not having a bit of my apology. "Girl, I've been everywhere. Done everything. Do you know how hard it is to surprise me? It's impossible. I thought the world was devoid of wonder. I thought it was over for me. But this Christmas? You two have shown me that there is still magic in the world."

I can't look over at Wes now. I know if I do, I'll burst into tears.

"I carry my own little holiday with me. Something I learned to do over the years." Margo reaches down to lift an old-fashioned makeup case, upholstered in green floral canvas, up onto the table. She clicks the brass snaps open.

I watch in wonder as she pulls out a small Christmas tree, complete with a green wooden stand. She sets it on the table between us and smiles over at Wes and me. "I have my favorite ornaments as well, the most special ones I've collected over the years."

I lean back in my seat, surprised to find Wes there,

having scooted close enough to put his arm around my shoulders. I hesitate for a moment and then relax back into him.

Margo lifts out a little ballerina and hangs it on the tiny tree. "This was my favorite from when I was a girl. The only thing I still have from those days."

I'm close to tears as she lifts out a few more, from her travels, gifts from dear friends, completely enthralled by this whole new side of Margo. I never would have thought she had a sentimental bone in her grumpy old body, but boy was I wrong.

"And this one." She lifts out a small brass skeleton key on a red satin ribbon. "Was a gift from my late husband after we bought our very first home."

She holds it out. "I want you to have it."

It's clear she means me, and I panic. "Margo, I can't take—"

"Hush. You two gave me the gift of knowing love isn't dead in this world. I want to give you something in return."

I reach out to take the little key, the metal cool between my fingers. "Thank you. I'll hang it somewhere special."

"You'll hang it on the tree in your own home," she responds.

I nod, even though it's hard to imagine when or how I'll ever have a real home of my own.

Next, she pulls out a small, golden treasure chest, studded with glass rubies and emeralds. "This one's for you."

Wes, having just watched me get shut down trying to refuse the gift, reaches out to take it immediately. "Thank you."

"Bing Crosby himself gave me that ornament. It was at a holiday party in New York, back when the world was still glamorous. He told me I could use it to hold my treasure.

And now, so can you. You never know what you may find in there."

I sit up and turn to watch Wes examining his new ornament. He holds it tightly and pulls the tiny-hinged lid open. His eyebrows raise just a bit, and his gaze darts to Margo before he smiles and closes it again, tucking it into his pocket. "I'll never squander it."

He holds my gaze for a long moment, the look in his eyes familiar, but I'm not quite able to place it. When his face melts into a smile, however, I know exactly what he's feeling. The same warm, calm contentment I've been puzzling over all morning.

There's no giant tree overflowing with perfectly wrapped gifts.

No roaring fire or fancy dinner to look forward to.

No stockings or mistletoe.

But somehow, this moment is enough.

We spend the rest of the day lounging by the pool, swimming, napping, and eating the delicious food Wes cooks for us on the barbeque. Wes suggests a Christmas beach walk after dinner to watch the sunset from the point, but Margo tells us she's too tired. I walk her to her room.

"Good night, dear," she tells me, door already half closed.

I smile because I'm pretty sure it's the first time she's called me something other than girl. Dear is almost a term of endearment. I feel like I won the game somehow.

"Good night, Margo. Merry Christmas."

"Thank you for everything. Both of you."

She closes the door before I can respond.

NOW'S NOT THE TIME FOR GAMES

WES

I FOLLOW Julia up the stairs, slowly, a step or two behind. Her unspoken invitation hangs in the air between us. Tonight already feels different.

She stops in front of her room and turns back to me, eyes sparkling with the magic of the day. I feel it, too.

"This is the first time I've ever invited you in," she jokes as I step closer until my chest is pressed to hers.

Julia leans forward to brush her lips across my collarbone. Sheer need courses through my veins so hard, I wonder if I'm vibrating.

I hear the key click against the lock, and she takes a step back into the room as the door swings open. I follow her inside, keeping my body pressed right up against hers. As soon as the door falls shut behind us, I find her lips, warm and soft, and tasting sweet from the tea we had after dessert.

It feels as though I've been starved my whole life up

until this point, and now? All I need is the taste of Julia on my lips.

She pulls back and steps across the room, setting her phone down on the coffee table before facing me once more where I stand.

Her face betrays the same thing I'm feeling. It's sure but unsure. An uncertain certainty.

"What's the game tonight, Santa and his elf?" she offers lightly, though I can hear what she's really asking.

Is this real?

I shake my head. "No game."

Her eyebrows rise, and I watch her chest rise as well and catch there.

The distance is killing me, so I cross the room to stand at her back, head draped over her shoulder.

"No spicy scene picked out?" she whispers.

I spin her to face me. "Tonight, I'm the author."

Julia holds her breath as I trace my fingers down her arms, circling her wrists where the sleeves of her work shirt are rolled up. I bring each of her hands up to my lips and kiss the backs, then kiss my way down her arms.

"Am I the coauthor?" she asks, breathless.

I move to kissing her collarbone and down to the dip between her breasts as I start to unbutton her shirt.

"You, wife, are the book."

I scoop her off her feet without warning and smile to myself as she cries out and then laughs, kicking her feet so her black pumps fall off as I carry her into the bedroom.

Tossing her on the bed, I stand over her, pulling my own shirt over my head and tossing it to the side.

She lies where I placed her, navy skirt riding up, half-buttoned white blouse coming untucked.

Reaching over, I pull out the chopstick holding her bun

in place and watch her long hair fall. "Do you know what this uniform of yours does to me?" I growl.

She shakes her head innocently, blinking up at me with long black lashes.

I pull one of her hands toward me, running her fingers along the length of my erection through my pants.

Her tongue darts out to lick her lips, and I'm a goner.

I'll never be able to focus on anything again as long as I live without the image of her like this flashing through my mind, distracting me.

"Is it the lipstick?" she asks.

I nod. "It's the lipstick." I reach down and roll her onto her side, landing a soft smack on the round swell of her ass. "It's these lacy panty lines under your tight skirt."

I run one of my hands over her ankle and up her calf. "It's your tan, smooth legs." I reach her knees and let my touch soften as I graze up her thigh. "It's the soft, blonde hair on your thighs."

My hand continues upward until I've got her hipbone in my grip, skirt shoved up high on her thighs, giving me the first peek of her red lace undies. "It's the fact that no matter how incredible I imagine you're going to look under this skirt. How incredible I imagine you're going to taste." I lean down to lick the damp scrap of fabric between her legs. She gasps and lets her legs drop open. "How incredible I imagine you're going to feel. You're so much more."

I find the nearly hidden zipper along the back of the skirt and control myself long enough to slip it down rather than tearing it off her. Unhooking the last of her blouse buttons, she's laid open before me, matching red lace panties and bra, white blouse hanging from her shoulders. Red lips open just enough to invite me inside.

I reach up to cup her chin and run my thumb across her bottom lip, slipping it into her mouth and hooking it over her bottom teeth. I pull her toward me with the grip, watching with erotic satisfaction as she obeys, bringing her body up to her knees, sitting on her heels.

"I want to taste you," she slurs a bit around my thumb in her mouth.

"Is that so?"

She nods eagerly.

I release her and let my hands fall to my sides.

She grasps my belt buckle like she really does want this as much as I do, which doesn't seem possible. The level of want I've reached doesn't feel like something I'm going to survive.

Like I'm going to die of watching her, of craving her, of having her.

Hell of a way to go.

Julia frees my cock and takes it in both hands, gripping the base as she pops the tip right into her mouth.

I gasp at the sudden contact, reaching up to grip her hair, just to have something tethering me to this world. "Shit, that's so good."

She slides me in deeper, and it's all I can do to let her have control. Not to thrust into her. I rock my hips slightly as she starts to suck and slide, and she allows it, leaning in even closer to take my tip further back. I can feel her throat swallowing as she licks up the underside of my shaft.

The red of her bra and panties, the red of her now smeared lips, the red of her cheeks as she feeds me in and out of her mouth.

My vision starts to blur with the pleasure of it all.

"It's my turn," I tell her, my voice coming out hoarse, like I'm in the middle of the sexiest blow job of my life. Which is certainly the case.

Julia nods eagerly, hands gripping me tighter as she starts to work me faster in and out of her lips.

"No," I say, pulling out quickly, just in time.

I have to catch my breath for a moment before I can speak again. "That's not what I meant."

I gesture with my chin. "On your back."

I take my time stripping her undies off with my teeth. It's been less than twenty-four hours since her bare pussy was in my face in the shower, but I still fall on it like a man starved, sucking an orgasm out of her straightaway. No waiting. Her taste fills my mouth, and I drink her down.

I wipe my drenched fingers on my aching cock, almost accidentally taking myself over the edge with the slippery contact. At the sight of Julia, panting before me, knees bent, legs splayed wide open. Like my own perfect Christmas present, unwrapped and ready to wrap around me.

"Did you like it when I filled you up last night, wife?" I don't know what's come over me. I'm a madman.

Julia's eyes go wide as she meets my gaze.

For a moment, I wonder if I've gone too far.

But then she nods.

"You liked being claimed?" I whisper.

She nods again.

"You're mine," I tell her. "Say it."

"I'm yours."

The slide into her is tight and hot and wet.

Julia moans as I stretch her open. "Don't stop."

"I never will." I mean it.

Her fingernails digging into my shoulders speak volumes. She can feel that it's the truth.

I know the girl likes it rough, and I deliver, bringing both myself and her right to the edge before pulling out and flipping her, giving my cock a moment to settle down and Julia a moment to follow my order to hold the headboard with both hands.

The angle of taking her from behind while she kneels

there, body stretched long before me as she grips the metal bar of the bed like it's the rock in a storm, it changes the chemistry of my brain. I release her hips and run my hands up the plane of her back as I thrust, touching every inch of her I can reach. Losing track of where my skin ends and hers begins.

Unable to edge myself again, I come inside her, recklessly, my heart close to exploding as I feel my fluid merge with hers. It's primal, an instinctual, animalistic act, and the cry that escapes my lips sounds more like a creature than myself. Wild. Visceral. Satisfied.

I can't make myself pull out, so I pull her body to mine, sitting her on my lap. We gasp in unison at the way the angle shifts. The new depth I find as she comes upright, leaning back against my body.

"Come for me, wife," I growl into the crook of her neck as I wrap my arm around to sink my fingers into the warm, wet folds of her.

I can tell by her ragged breathing that she's close already, and I give her the pressure she wants to ride, closing my eyes as the pleasure of her hips rocking gently back and forth threatens to bring me to climax once more.

When she comes, body tightening around mine, I may as well be coming alongside her. Her held breath is my held breath. Her pleasure seeps out of her body in a wave, taking me under.

I don't ever want to let her go, but after a long moment of breathing, dripping together, she wiggles out of my arms. My still half-hard cock releases as she slides down to lie before me.

I lock gazes with her for the first time since I started taking her from behind. I can't look away. Julia holds my stare, offering the windows of her soul to me, flung wide open.

Curling beside her, I hold her like that. Gaze-to-gaze, feeling myself more and more lost in the depths of her, until her eyes finally blink, blink, and fall closed.

"Merry Christmas," I whisper.

Julia smiles sleepily. "This is the best one I've ever had."

"It feels like the only one I've ever had," I answer honestly.

Her eyes crack open, and she peers out at me once more. "The only one?"

"The first one," I tell her. "I feel like I was born right in this moment."

"We'll have to get you one of those first Christmas ornaments," she jokes softly as her eyes close.

I smile to myself at the humor, but she'll get no argument here.

My whole life has been spent searching. Waiting, wishing.

If someone had told me just a few months ago that all I needed was to take the leap of faith and the universe would be waiting below with a net, I wouldn't have believed them.

But here I am. Sharing Christmas night with the love of my life. Preparing to break my world wide open and step out on the other side a changed man.

Rule #11

TAKE THE DAMN LEAP

JULIA

MY WHOLE BODY glows with pheromones and hormones and happiness as we make our way down the stairs to the main floor to get started on breakfast before Margo wakes up. She's been sleeping until nearly nine the last few days, so we pushed it a bit later than usual, getting to the lobby area at eight thirty.

Wes breaks off for the kitchen, planting a kiss directly on my lips before he goes, sending me straight back into the pleasure haze of the night before.

It's one hundred percent due to this distracted state that I fail to see the problem before it's staring straight at me, hands on hips.

"What exactly is going on here?" Sam asks.

"Oh!" I stop in my tracks, smoothing down my hair and skirt, thanking the gods of good choices that I put on my work uniform today, even after three days of Wes teasing me for being so formal. "We...I..." I clear my throat. "I tried to text you."

Sam pulls out his phone and glances down at the screen, and then up at me. This man is nothing if not fair, gentle, and kind. But I can see that he's struggling to stay calm right now.

"Text me about what?" His tone is cautious, reserved.

"We had a guest arrive last minute. Someone who didn't get the message about the resort being closed."

His eyebrows raise. He doesn't believe me.

I panic. "It was Margo Vale."

"Margo?"

I nod, confidence returning slightly as I offer up a piece of information he seems to find important. "She just walked up with her suitcase and expected her room to be ready. I didn't know what to do, but I didn't think you'd want me to turn her away, so I—"

"Threw her a Christmas?"

I cough out a laugh that sounds far more maniacal than I intend. It comes with the threat of what absolutely cannot be nervous tears. I suck in a deep breath to get a hold of myself so I can explain.

"We did our best to make her comfortable with the power outage and...everything."

"We?" Sam asks.

I don't need to answer.

At that moment, Chef Dominic marches down the hallway from the kitchens, Wes following behind him like a man on death row. "I found a stowaway," he offers in what could be a joking tone for Dominic—terrifying but upbeat.

Sam huffs out a laugh and shakes his head. "So did I. Mine's got a story, though."

"That a famous reporter showed up at the last minute demanding an ocean front room and a full holiday experience?"

Sam nods. "Yeah."

"Well, like I told Wes. If he can produce Margo Vale, he's off the hook."

Sam turns to me. "Where is she staying?"

I perk up, happy for the prospect of this tense interaction ending and Margo explaining everything to my angry bosses. "Room one twelve."

Sam nods again. "Lead the way."

I knock softly on Margo's door. "Good morning, Ms. Vale. Coffee's ready."

There's no answer.

I knock again.

Still nothing.

I feel the three men in the hallway behind me like a boulder of tension, waiting to crush me flat. "Maybe she's in the shower."

Sam holds up his master key, gesturing for me to step aside. I do, of course. He's the boss. And I have nothing to fear here. Our story is true.

"Housekeeping," Sam calls as he swings the door open and peeks his head into the room.

I'm praying she's not in there naked.

Turns out, I should have been praying for myself.

After a moment, Sam swings the door wide open.

The room is empty.

The bed is made.

There's no luggage in sight.

I hurry into the suite, looking left and right, hand clasped over my wide-open mouth like a scandalized fifties movie star. "But...she..."

Spinning around, I find Wes's confused face. "Where is

she?" I ask, more worried for the old woman in this moment than I am for the fate of my job.

He just shakes his head.

"What's this?" Dominic asks, pushing his way into the room. "No secret VIP guest? Just you two shacking up in the resort while we were all away?"

I open my mouth to protest, horror turning my blood to ice.

But Sam holds up his hand to stop me. "We don't have enough information to make that call yet, Dom. But..." He turns to me, stripping away my temporary relief. "We're also going to need some way to verify that what you are saying is true. Without a guest to vouch for you, this all looks pretty bad."

Even backed against the wall, being forced to consider terminating two employees for lying, stealing, and trespassing, Sam still maintains his diplomacy.

"She was here," I insist. "She came three days ago. We only had our own groceries and battery-powered lights, but we made her stay as comfortable as we could. We made her a lovely Christmas. We even took her out—"

Wes catches my eye and drags a finger across his throat. *Shut your mouth, Julia.*

"To...to the orchard," I stammer, thanking Wes with my gaze for stopping me from telling the owners of the resort that we commandeered a boat.

"She...she was happy." My final plea comes out sounding a bit tearful, and I vow to quit while I'm ahead.

"That very well may be. And we'll thank you for doing what you could to make an important guest comfortable—" Sam starts.

"But until then." Dom steps into the room, arms crossed over his chest. "You two better go home."

Sam nods. "We know where to find you if we have any

other…questions," Sam says, glancing around the room once more.

Wes grabs my arms and pulls me from the room. It might not be the most appropriate gesture, considering the circumstances, but I'm grateful. I don't know if I could have managed to walk away on my own. To leave when my future is still hovering in the air, dead or alive.

We hurry up the back staircase to the second floor and shove my belongings into the few bags I brought as quickly as we can. Wes slips both of the little ornaments into his pocket and holds the door open for me.

"What about your stuff?" I ask.

He shakes his head. "I'll get it later. Or not."

I open my mouth to protest, but he's already leading me back down the stairs and through the lobby. I feel the concerned gaze of the two resort owners on our backs as we push our way through the front doors and out into the warm morning.

"You can come to my house," I tell him. "For now."

Forever, I want to say. But I'm not sure about anything right now, so it feels heavy to make promises. Everything that I thought I knew, all my plans for the future, now seem so tenuous.

What if I no longer have a job? Will I even want to live across the street from a resort that fired me?

"Do you have coffee?" Wes asks.

He grinds the beans and gets the pot brewing while I pace back and forth, both hands gripping my hair at the scalp, freaking the fuck out. "We should go back over there."

"They told us to leave."

"But what if Margo's in trouble? Where could she have gone?"

He sets a steaming cup down on the table and leads me

over to it, sitting me down with a gentle press on my shoulders. "What was the last thing she said to you?"

I think back to the night before. "She called me dear," I answer, biting my lip.

And then it hits me.

"And she said thank you for everything. Both of you. That's what she said. 'Thank you for everything, both of you.'"

Wes grimaces. "Okay, so she was already planning her silent exit."

"But why?"

He shrugs. "She gave us our gifts. She said thank you. I guess she was done with us."

I can't let it go. "What if she walked down to the water and fell in? What if she's just floating out there?"

Wes pulls me close. "I'm sorry it didn't work out the way you were hoping. With your promotion and whatnot."

I tense up at the loaded word.

Promotion.

It's carried a lot of weight for me over the years. It's been the North Star guiding my whole life. Just move up. Keep moving up. As if some paradise could be found at the top.

What a fool I've been.

The last three days have been the happiest, most fun of my entire life. And I'm just a lowly front desk agent.

"I had the number for the caretakers from Merit Island," I blurt out, mostly to quiet my spiraling mind. "I should have called them to help. I could have called the cruise company from my home landline. I could have done so many things. But I wanted to be the hero. And now look where it's gotten us. Fired."

I hang my head in the silence that follows my shameful admission. I'm sure Wes is pissed. I wouldn't blame him if he ran back over there and told them it was all my fault.

It would be the truth.

"The generator techs tried to come turn the power back on."

It takes me a long moment to process his words.

I raise my head and narrow my eyes at him. "What do you mean?"

He shrugs sheepishly. "I found a note on the door before we went snorkeling. They needed access to the property to reset the generators."

"And you just got on the boat and didn't say anything? Left the place locked so they couldn't get in?" I think back to that morning, racking my brain to find any indication from Wes that he was holding a secret.

But all I can remember is the gentle, intimate moment on the beach.

When he admitted to being as lonely as I am.

When he made me choose a safe word.

"I didn't want them to turn it on. I wanted...well, Jules, I wanted you."

I laugh softly and shake my head. "We really are a couple of poor decision makers."

"Or masters of our own destinies," he replies.

I want to be able to see this all in the same light as Wes, but I'm still too shocked by the turn of events and ashamed of being caught by the same bosses I was trying so hard to impress.

I take a sip of my coffee, and it sinks, bitter and acidic, into my empty belly. "I'm starving."

"We didn't get to make our Boxing Day omelets."

"All of my groceries are over there. My fridge is empty."

Wes pushes to his feet, placing a kiss on the top of my head. "Let's head to town."

I nod, reaching into the basket on the table and pulling out my keys. "I'll drive."

"You have a golf cart?" Wes asks in surprise.

"Of course, don't you?"

He shakes his head, heading out to the front yard.

I narrow my eyes at him as I lock the front door. "No vehicle and sleeping illegally in the basement at work. But still collecting what is no doubt a pretty good paycheck. What are you hoarding money for? Paying off mobsters?"

Wes just winks at me with a mischievous smile. "When we get to town, I'll show you."

Rule #12

PLOT TWIST: HAPPILY EVER AFTER

WES

WE PARK at Mackenzie's and walk down Main Street. By some unspoken agreement, we don't hold hands but walk close enough for our arms to touch.

Downtown Saubry Village is still decorated to the nines with tropical holiday decor, making it feel like walking into a Jimmy Buffett song.

Mr. Harlan steps out on the porch of his bakery as we pass, waving hello. "Missed you yesterday. But it looks like you had other plans." His smile is wide and joyful.

I can't help but smile back, for so many reasons. "Good to see you."

"I've got some leftovers from the party yesterday, if you two are hungry."

Julia's eyes light up. "Starving."

As a dedicated chef and culinarian, feeding people has always been my favorite hobby. I can see now that feeding Julia is quickly becoming my new obsession.

Mr. Harlan holds the screen door open for us as we

come inside. "Croissant or sticky bun?" he asks, heading behind the counter.

"Both," I answer, tilting sideways just enough to tap Julia's shoulder gently with mine. She glances over at me, bashful smile grazing her lips as she reaches for my hand.

We leave with a treat for now, and two for later. Julia starts to turn on the little side street that leads to Island Market, but when I keep going straight, she backtracks and chases me down the dusty street.

"Where are you taking me?"

"I told you I'd show you my secret."

"Ooh, I can't wait!"

She doesn't have to wait long.

Right before we reach the edge of the sandy beach, I stop short and turn to face a small, wooden building, blue paint chipped but still bright. It doesn't look like much now, but I know just inside the shuttered front window is a row of shiny new stainless appliances, a fridge and freezer, and prep table with a brand-new white cutting board. Out back is the real show—a propane rotisserie, charcoal grill, and wood-fired smoker.

From where we stand, facing the closed window with its faded white wooden counter and blank round sign on the side where the last owners painted over their logo, I feel the need to explain.

But Julia seems to get it right away. "Is this what you've been saving up for?" she asks excitedly, turning to me, eyes wide.

I nod. "I made the final payment last week. I get the keys tomorrow, when the owners are back from the mainland."

"It's perfect! Oh my gosh. You'll be able to do so much with it. And right on the beach." Julia rushes forward, examining the counter and the door and heading around back.

With a laugh, I follow her. We spend a while checking out the outdoor appliances, Julia listening with rapt attention as I tell her what they're for and what my plans are for the space. "I'm going to call it Slowburn."

She laughs. "Unlike our little romance?"

I shrug, feeling timid all of a sudden to admit how long I've been watching her strut around the resort in her tight work skirt and cute black heels. "Hopefully Slowburn has the same success written in the stars."

Julia narrows her eyes at me. "What do you mean hopefully? Wes, this location and your talent? It's going to be a smashing success. Are you really concerned?"

It's a hard question to answer.

Last week, when I made the last payment to complete the most expensive purchase of my life, I'd been completely alone. I hadn't told any of my coworkers at the resort about the project for fear they'd try to take it from me. Or told my bosses, who I had yet to give my notice.

My plan was to quietly move out of the resort and into the backroom of Slowburn, doing just the basics to get open and start slinging meat out the front counter, building the menu over time as I became able to buy more ingredients and pay more bills.

It's only been a few days, but already everything feels different.

I have someone who believes in me, maybe even more than I believe in myself.

"I have been on quite the lucky streak lately," I respond, pulling her close and planting my lips on hers. The way she softens in my arms, melting into my body, nearly takes my breath away. Her lips part, and I graze my tongue slowly over hers, savoring the sweet, salty, Julia taste. "But I can't help but worry how it will all look when the holiday magic wears off."

Julia tilts her head up to face me, still wrapped tightly in my arms. "I think I have just the cure for that."

She walks over to the far side of the small building and stands next to a young tree about the same height she is, holding out both hands as if unveiling a shiny new car. "Christmas forever!"

I laugh as I see her point. The Norfolk Island pine looks as close to a traditional pine as you can find in a place like this. And the fact that it's just growing here, in the backyard of my new place, does feel a bit like magic.

I walk over to join her, slipping the two ornaments out of my pocket. I hand her the key, and she hangs it on one of the branches.

When I hold up my own ornament, however, I don't hang it up right away. Holding it between my thumb and forefinger, I pry open the lid of the treasure chest and lift out the prize Margo hid there for me.

Julia gasps when she sees it.

The simple diamond solitaire ring.

I drop down to one knee, grinning up at my very shocked future wife. "What do you say? Want to become my real captive bride so I can spend the rest of our lives spoiling you with the fortunes from my meat shack?"

Tears well up in her eyes as she continues to stare down at me, hands clasped over her mouth. "Wes, this is crazy," she says finally, a trail of—hopefully—happy tears escaping to roll down her cheeks as she speaks.

"Yup," I agree. "But so was squatting in the basement of the resort while I sublet my apartment to save up enough to pay cash for a restaurant on the beach. Maybe I'm crazy. But I think you're a little crazy, too. And I'm crazy in love with you."

Her hands drop to her sides as she lets out her breath and shakes her head side-to-side in disbelief. "I can't believe I'm about to say this."

My own eyes drop closed in anticipation.

"Yes."

Never in all my years would I have guessed that one simple word could make everything fall into place. But here we are.

I slip the ring onto Julia's outstretched finger. A perfect fit. Yet another sign from the universe that this was meant to be. I place a kiss on the back of her hand and gaze up into her eyes. "Wife."

She pulls me to my feet and sinks into my arms once more. "Not quite yet. We still have a restaurant to open before we can even begin to think about planning a wedding."

I pull back just enough to meet her gaze. "We?"

She scoffs. "Yes, we. You're going to need to be slinging a lot of meat from this shack to properly take care of me. You don't think I'm going to let you do that alone, do you? Who's going to get everything properly arranged and greet the guests and call out the orders? Who's going to make sure you eat lunch and drink water while you're up to your ears in tickets all day?"

I could not be happier if the sky opened up and rained hundred-dollar bills. "Who's going to assign herself a nice, short skirt for her work uniform and lean over the counter to hand out orders?" I slide both hands up her thighs, pushing her navy-blue work skirt from The Sands up until I have her full ass in my grasp. "And distract me from my work?"

Julia squeals and tries to escape, but I hold her tightly against me.

Until our joyous struggle is interrupted by a loud, deliberate throat clearing behind me.

Julia looks over my shoulder and pulls away, taking a step back and smoothing down her skirt.

I spin around to find the mischievous smile of Margo Vale.

"Am I interrupting something?"

"Just celebrating," I answer, at the same time Julia exclaims, "You're alive!"

Margo scoffs. "Of course I'm alive." But then her face softens. "Sorry to sneak out on you like that. I've never been one for goodbyes."

"We'd appreciate it if you called out to The Sands," I tell her, saying what Julia is clearly too polite to admit. "They didn't believe us when we told them a surprise guest showed up. With you gone, it sort of looked like we were camping out there, throwing ourselves a Christmas party."

"Well, my review posted half an hour ago. They'll be thanking you soon enough."

As soon as she says it, I hear Julia's phone ding. Mine buzzes in my pocket. I pull it out to find a text from Dom. It's just a screenshot from *The New York Times* article.

The hospitality at The White Sands Resort restored my faith in the entire industry. Never have I felt so welcomed or have staff shown so much heart making sure I was comfortable and enjoyed my holiday. I'd come to the conclusion over the last decade that no one cared anymore. I stand before you now, corrected. If you can manage to secure a reservation at this tropical beach paradise, you won't regret it. You have my word on that.

A text message follows shortly after.

DOM

Good work.

I laugh and tuck my phone away. I can tell by the look on Julia's face she got a similar text. And that it might complicate things.

"I don't mind if you—" I start letting her off the hook.

But Julia just shakes her head, cutting me off. "Not now, okay? Today we celebrate you."

"Us," I reply, holding her hand up to my lips once more.

We both turn to face Margo as she lets out a contented sigh.

"That ring brought me the happiest years of my entire life. I wish you two the same."

Julia's face widens in surprise, and I worry she's going to try to give the ring back to Margo. But in the end, she just offers a heartfelt, "Thank you."

Margo shakes her head. "You can thank me by letting me know when you get this place running so I can be your first customer."

I grin at her. "You'd fly over from New York for that?"

The old lady just shrugs mysteriously. "Or maybe the owner of a certain beach bungalow will accept my offer, and I'll be spending more time on Faraday Island."

She tips her wide-brimmed hat and disappears around the corner before either of us can congratulate her.

Once we're alone again, Julia spins to face me. "You tried to give her the ring back, right?"

"Of course," I assure her. "And you can imagine exactly how that went."

She smiles and huffs out a laugh. "Yeah, I can."

But then she turns pensive. "You know, I've spent so long working toward promotions and career advancement, wondering if that's really all there is to life. I thought I needed success to be recognized. To be loved. I didn't realize I could be myself. Just find joy in the small pleasures of my life. Create my home where I already am and allow myself to be happy there. I was repeating the same old pattern at my job at The Sands. Desperately trying to use work to give my life meaning. Then that woman strolled up the drive and delivered the one gift I never would have even known to ask for."

"What's that, wife?"

Julia grins at me. "A Christmas plot twist."

A Look At: Off the Menu

—OFF-LIMITS LOVERS BOOK ONE—

He says I'm his good girl... but why does it feel like I'm his dirty little secret?

I came to this island for a clean slate. No drama. No distractions. Just a job, some sunshine, and a chance to finally get my life back on track.

Then I met him—my infuriating, devastatingly hot boss.

He's older. Untouchable. Completely off-limits.

And somehow, I'm the one he can't stay away from.

Behind closed doors, he's all dominance and dirty promises. But in the daylight? He keeps me at arm's length—and our relationship under wraps.

What starts as heat becomes something more…or at least, I think it does. But love doesn't look like hiding. And secrets don't feel like safety. So when the line between pleasure and pain starts to blur, I have to ask myself: Is this real—or am I just a beautiful, temporary escape?

AVAILABLE NOW

Lore Townsend writes "feelings-forward spice"—steamy, emotionally rich romance full of messy characters, complicated connections, and hard-won happily ever afters. With a background in psychology and a past life slinging drinks while eavesdropping on disastrous first dates, she's always been fascinated by how we love—and what happens when it all goes sideways.

She lives on a rainy little island in the Pacific Northwest, where deer savage her gardens and the Wi-Fi never quite cooperates. When she's not writing, she's pulling tarot cards, daydreaming in the shower, or manifesting her next beachside "research" trip. She's the author of eight romance novels and just getting warmed up.

www.loretownsend.com
Join Lore Townsend's Romance Club

www.ingramcontent.com/pod-product-compliance
Lightning Source LLC
Chambersburg PA
CBHW010828250626
47169CB00010B/2996